CRIME WAVES 1

CRIME WAVES 1.

The Annual Anthology of the
Crime Writers' Association

edited by

H. R. F. KEATING

LONDON
VICTOR GOLLANCZ LTD
1991

First published in Great Britain 1991
by Victor Gollancz Ltd
14 Henrietta Street, London WC2E 8QJ

© Victor Gollancz Ltd 1991

er 23.95/13.10 - 4/92

A catalogue record for this book
is available from the British Library

ISBN 0–575–05171–X
ISBN 0–575–05172–8 pbk

Typeset at The Spartan Press Ltd,
Lymington, Hampshire
Printed by Mackays of Chatham plc,
Chatham, Kent

CONTENTS

Acknowledgements 7

Foreword by H. R. F. Keating 9

Antonia Fraser: Getting to Know You 13

Michael Gilbert: Blood Match 25

Catherine Aird: The Hard Sell 34

Peter Lovesey: The Corder Figure 41

Margaret Yorke: The Mouse Will Play 59

Susan Moody: Poisoned Tongues 67

Liza Cody: K. K. 81

Simon Brett: Letter to his Son 88

Reginald Hill: Urban Legend 104

Robert Barnard: Happy Christmas 110

Herbert Harris: Bad Move 122

David Williams: Something to Declare 126

Michael Z. Lewin: Danny Gets it Right 142

Julian Symons: The Tiger's Stripe 149

Mike Ripley: Our Man Marlowe 168

Paula Gosling: The Perfect Alibi 174

H. R. F. Keating: A Snaking Suspicion 185

ACKNOWLEDGEMENTS

Original stories in this collection are 'The Hard Sell' by Catherine Aird, 'Danny Gets it Right' by Michael Z. Lewin, and 'Our Man Marlowe' by Mike Ripley. Acknowledgements are due to *Murder and Company* (Pandora) for 'K. K.' by Liza Cody; *Sisters in Crime* (Berkeley, USA) for 'Getting to Know You' by Antonia Fraser; *Metropolis* magazine for 'Blood Match' by Michael Gilbert; *Winter's Crimes 17* (Macmillan) for 'The Perfect Alibi' by Paula Gosling; *Winter's Crimes 18* (Macmillan) for 'Letter to his Son' by Simon Brett; *Amateur Gardening* magazine for 'Bad Move' by Herbert Harris; *Butchers and Other Stories of Crime* (Macmillan) for 'The Corder Figure' by Peter Lovesey; *Ladykillers* (Dent) for 'The Mouse Will Play' by Margaret Yorke; and *Ellery Queen's Mystery Magazine* for 'Happy Christmas' by Robert Barnard, 'Urban Legend' by Reginald Hill, 'A Snaking Suspicion' by H. R. F. Keating, 'Poisoned Tongues' by Susan Moody, 'The Tiger's Stripe' by Julian Symons, and 'Something to Declare' by David Williams.

FOREWORD

All human life is there. That's what you get when you ask a band from the Crime Writers' Association for stories they rank among their best. But you get something else, too. You get precisely stories. Words laid out so as to keep you reading while you count the ways of what that magnificent American storyteller the late Stanley Ellin once called 'that streak of wickedness in human nature'.

So in Antonia Fraser's 'Getting to Know You' we have, despite outward appearances, what politics can do in the way of wickedness, as we meet once again (Hurrah!) Jemima Shore, TV interviewer, a figure so much of our times it is difficult to remember she is in fact no more than a figment of her creator's imagination. Or, in 'Blood Match', we get to see whole varieties of decades-old wickedness so to speak, legal-side-up. No one writes better of the many wrinkles of the law than Michael Gilbert, and no one knows better how to give us readers the sort of story where you don't just want to know what happens in the end but you want to know what happens in the next paragraph and the next and the next.

If Michael Gilbert's tale takes us back to a distant but not dim past, Catherine Aird's 'The Hard Sell' shows us wickedness flaunted very much amid our own greed-ridden times. And, as you are moved irresistibly along its course, revel (as I did) in the delicious little darts of wit you encounter, like morsels of mushroom enlivening a sustaining steak pie. But, if Catherine Aird intrigues us by asking 'How could he possibly have . . . ?', Peter Lovesey in 'The Corder Figure' intrigues us every bit as much with quite different questions: 'What on earth are they playing at?' and 'Who's playing with whom?', and when you learn the answers what do you get but a last line that in three words doubles your pleasure.

Three 'Village mysteries' in the stories Margaret Yorke, Susan Moody and Reginald Hill give us. In 'The Mouse Will Play', with its plot and counter-plot among the everyday details of life on a 'nice' estate very much of our day, it might seem there is hardly any crime at all. But, no, that wicked streak is really as much to the fore there as it is when sawn-off shotguns blast or feet are jammed in concrete boots. In Susan Moody's 'Poisoned Tongues', where we are in an actual cottages-crammed village, the crimes are equally quiet but just as quivering with wickedness. Not for nothing did Rebecca West once say 'Blackmail is the iciest sin'. And, despite his title, 'Urban Legend', Reginald Hill's diabolically cunning piece of story-spinning needs for its full effect the smiling and beautiful countryside which, as Sherlock Holmes told us long ago, presents a more dreadful record of sin than the lowest and vilest alleys.

All sorts of wickedness in Simon Brett's 'Letter to His Son'. But it is laid on with such an insouciant touch that you simply don't take it in as grievous bodily harm, drug smuggling, confidence trickery or what-have-you. Instead you enjoy the long, long running joke with a chuckle in its every turn and twist.

Then, as if to show the whole stretch of crime writing at its widest, we have Liza Cody's 'K. K.' where, in a disturbingly odd setting, a note of genuine tragedy is struck leaving one with more than a little to think about. While, if with Margaret Yorke and Susan Moody the streak of wickedness was at its lightest and thinnest, in Robert Barnard's 'Happy Christmas' – if you want an antidote to the jollifications swallow this down and try not to make a face – the streak is as thick as the sharpest cynic, or most level-headed of realists, could want.

It is a particular pleasure to me that this collection includes a story by Herbert Harris, 'Bad Move', typically brief, typically neat. Herbert, a former Chairman of the Crime Writers' Association, and the only one of us (I think) to gain a place in the *Guinness Book of Records* – it was as writer of over 3,000 short stories – edited our annual anthology from 1966 right up until well-earned retirement last year. A hundred writers and more have cause to be grateful to him.

Two stories take their springing-point from real-life people, though I hesitate, since one of them is very much alive, to add 'and their real-life wickednesses'. With Mike Ripley's 'Our Man Marlowe' – first spritzer of surprise hidden in the very title – we are on safe ground, however, as he ingeniously points out to us that wickedness is an unchanging factor in the human psyche from Elizabethan times to our own. I am not sure that the wickedness in Michael Z. Lewin's 'Danny Gets it Right' doesn't reside in the author who has dangled for our delight someone we ought, if we too were not a little wicked, deeply to respect. But his story is so tear-streamingly funny that I, for one, can easily forgive him the naughtiness.

Three stories remarkable for their solid, on-going narration. David Williams gives us in 'Something to Declare' a tale in which the pleasure lies in the intricate manoeuvrings of the plot, and if it only takes advantage of our human propensity to wickedness to get just within the bounds of the probable we willingly suspend any disbelief for the pleasure of the punch-line. In Julian Symons' hands, with 'The Tiger's Stripe', we are caught up in a very different game. We are squarely in the area of psychological truth, however disquieting it may be, as he reveals what each one of us might come to do, or fail to do, if circumstances put us in the squirming dilemma that afflicted ordinary Bradley Fawcett. Paula Gosling in 'The Perfect Alibi' has adopted that most cunning of storytellers' ploys, the story told by a person in the story itself, and twist by delightful twist she takes us with her yarn-spinner on to the beautifully unsuspected solution.

Finally, an apology. Or two even. First for having agreed to include a story of my own, 'A Snaking Suspicion', and, second, for that dreadful pun itself. But I can plead it is a sort of clue to the kind of story you will get, a bit of swift ingenuity and literary homage, based of course on a certain streak in human nature. And there is in the squib, too, a little extra puzzle for you. Not only does the villain share the name of a Conan Doyle character, but there to be spotted is a character from the work of another much-hailed crime novelist. No prizes, but good hunting.

GETTING TO KNOW YOU

Antonia Fraser

The moment the door was shut behind her, the man put the security chain across it. Then he ordered Jemima Shore to take her clothes off. All of her clothes.

'But you can leave your shoes on, if you like. They're pretty.'

Jemima found that the sheer unreality of the situation prevented her from taking in what he was saying. She could hear the words all right; the man was standing right beside her, his breath on her cheek – although he was not in fact breathing particularly heavily. They were about the same height: his eyes, very widely set, the colour of glossy chestnuts, were level with hers.

The man's hair was dark, very thick and quite long and shaggy; they were so close that she could see one or two silver threads in the dark mass. He had a moustache, sideburns, and soft dark down on his cheeks; it was that which gave him a Mediterranean look. His accent, however, faint but discernible, she could not place. He wore a clean white T-shirt with some kind of logo on it, and jeans. The broad shoulders and the heavy arms revealed by the contours of the T-shirt gave an impression of considerable physical strength, in spite of his calm breathing. Jemima was aware that he was sweating slightly.

She was carrying a large green Chanel-type handbag of quilted leather slung over her shoulder by two gilt chains. The man took the bag from her and put it carefully on the king-sized bed which dominated the hotel room. The curtains were drawn and the lamp by the bed was lit, although it was in fact only eleven o'clock in the morning.

The man repeated his command: 'Take off your clothes.' He added, 'I want to get to know you.'

It was idiotic, thought Jemima: the previous television programme she had worked on had actually been about rape. During that period, she had spoken to at least a dozen victims – of widely differing ages – on the subject. The words she had heard most frequently went something like this: 'You just don't understand what it's like . . . Helplessness . . . If it's never happened to you . . . Until it's happened to you . . .'

Naturally, she had never sought to argue the point. Her intention, as an investigative television reporter, had been to present her evidence as sympathetically but candidly as possible in order to illustrate just that gulf: between sufferers and the rest, however well intentioned. The programme about rape had been the last in a series of which the overall title had been *Twice Punished*: it had concentrated on the tragic social after-effects of certain crimes.

'Helplessness. . . You just don't understand . . . Until it happens to you.' Now it seemed Jemima was going to find out for herself the truth of those sad, despairing cries. Rather too late for her programme. Ironically enough. And she had a feeling she was going to need all the sense of irony (or detachment) she could hang on to in the present situation. And then something more.

'Take off your clothes,' repeated the man for the third time. 'I want to get to know you.' He was still not hurried or breathing heavily; only the slight perspiration on his upper lip betrayed any kind of agitation. Jemima now guessed him to be Moroccan or Algerian, maybe even Turkish; his actual use of English was more or less perfect.

'Who are you? And where is Clemency Vane? I have come to interview Clemency Vane.' Jemima decided the best course was to ignore the ludicrous frightening command altogether and attempt in some way to gain a mastery of the situation. She was glad to find that her own voice was absolutely steady even if she, unlike the man himself, was panting a little. She found that she was also able to manage a small, sweet, composed smile, the one the viewers loved, because Jemima generally went on to demolish the recipient of that sweet smile – some pompous political leader perhaps – politely but totally.

'Clemmie' – he accented the last syllable just slightly – 'is not here. I have come instead. Now you will take off your clothes please. Or' – he paused as if to consider the situation in a rational manner – 'I could perhaps take them off for you. But you would probably prefer to do it yourself.'

The man bent forward and undid the loose drawstring tie at the neck of Jemima's cream-coloured jersey dress. His hands, like his shoulders, were large and muscular: they were covered with dark hair; the nails, Jemima noticed automatically, were very clean, as if scrubbed, and well-kept. He undid the first pearl button and made as if to touch the second; then he drew back.

This is where I scream, thought Jemima. Argument stops here. There must be somebody in earshot in this damn barn of a hotel.

'Don't touch me, please,' she said aloud. 'And I must tell you that, whoever you are, my camera crew are due to arrive in this room in exactly one minute; they took the next lift.'

'Oh, don't be frightened.' The man ignored her remark about the camera crew which was in itself a worrying sign – since it was in fact quite untrue. Jemima doubted whether at this precise moment anyone in the world knew exactly where she was, not even Cherry, her faithful PA at Megalith Television.

'I'm not going to hurt you,' he said. 'Even if you scream – ' he had clearly read her mind – 'I shall not hurt you, only silence you with this.' For the first time Jemima realised the man was carrying a large white scarf or cloth on his arm. 'But please do not scream. There would be no point, I think, since both the rooms near us are empty, and the maid is far away.'

The man hesitated, then he led Jemima quite gently but firmly in the direction of the large bed. They both sat down. That brought her – possibly – within reach of her green handbag; but what kind of weapon was a soft quilted-leather handbag, however large? The man gazed at her earnestly with those wideapart brown eyes.

'I have seen you on television, Jemima. I think you're very beautiful and you're intelligent too. I like that very much. You'll find I really appreciate your intelligence when we get to know each other better. Women should cultivate their intelligence so as to be of interest to men; how can a stupid woman be of any interest to a man . . . ? Education is very important for women. In order to help their man.'

Now that the man was talking, almost rattling along, poking his face close to hers, talking at manic speed but not attempting otherwise to touch her or her clothing in any way, the best plan seemed to be to keep him at it.

The education of women! A bizarre subject to discuss, perhaps, under the present circumstances, but one on which Jemima did at least have strong views (if not precisely these views).

'You're absolutely right,' she agreed, her tone still resolutely equable, resisting the temptation to adjust the loose tie and button of her dress.

On the subject of education, would it be a good plan or a very bad plan to reintroduce the subject of Clemency Vane? Her captor – for such he was – either knew her or knew of her. As it was, one could indeed fruitfully talk about the education of Clemency Vane and at some length, in view of what had happened to her following that education. Had the missing Clemency been actually present in the hotel room where she promised to be, Jemima herself would have shot off some pertinent questions on the subject: even if she would have recorded the answers in her own well-trained memory (and not as yet with a camera crew). Clemency had asked for her to take no notes and certainly not use a tape recorder at these preliminary interviews. And Jemima, who at this stage was committed to nothing, Clemency having made all the running herself, had nothing to lose by agreeing to her terms.

Clemency Vane was a convicted criminal who had recently been released from prison where she had spent something over five years on a charge of drug dealing. It was an odd case. Nobody seemed to know quite where all the money had gone: some really large sums had vanished. Jemima remembered that the original sentence had been for eight years and that Clemency had been released for good behaviour: it had certainly been a strong sentence for a first offender. On the other hand the proven details of Clemency Vane's drug dealing were pretty strong too. And it was undeniably dealing: no question of a desperate addict merely trying to service her own expensive habit. Quite apart from the fact that she had pleaded guilty.

The oddness lay in the hint of political background to it all, a hint which mysteriously and totally disappeared when the case came to be tried and the 'guilty' plea was entered. What was the country concerned? Jemima tried to remember. Red Clemmie? Blue

Clemmie? Green Clemmie? Not the latter presumably in view of the drug dealing. Since none of this had finally been proffered by the defence at her trial, temporarily the name of the country eluded her: which was ridiculous. But she would have reminded herself of all the details of the case beforehand if Clemency Vane's summons to an interview in the anonymous barn of a West London hotel had not come so peremptorily to her this morning. That had altered their previous more long-term arrangements.

'No, it can't wait. I thought it could when I spoke to you originally. But now it can't.'

Santangela. That was it. Santangela: one of those little states, whose precise connection with drug traffic, anti-drug traffic measures, nationalism, and anti-imperialism was so difficult to establish even for those who were keenly interested. Which most Britons, and Jemima was no exception, frankly were not. That was the hint of political background which had come and then mysteriously gone away. After all, shortly after Clemency Vane had been imprisoned, there had been a successful revolution in Santangela in any case; so the whole situation had changed. Santangela: where exactly was the place? Latin America? Central America? South America? It was ridiculous to be so ignorant about sheer geography, which was after all a matter of fact. But then that was Europe-centred Britain – including Jemima Shore – for you.

Jemima looked at the man again. Not a Moroccan, an Algerian or a Turk, then, but a Santangelino? If that was what its nationals were called, as she seemed to remember they were. More vagueness, she ruefully admitted. All the same, for the first time her gaze was inquisitive, not challenging and self-protective. A Santangelino. Somehow connected to Clemency Vane's drug charge, once deemed in some way political, then all of a sudden quite apolitical, just criminal. What she was not in any way clear about as yet was exactly how Clemency and her drugs fitted into Jemima's current series. She had been wondering that ever since Clemency Vane had made the first contact. But there seemed plenty of time to find out.

Jemima's new series – very much at the planning stage – was tentatively entitled *For the Love of the Cause*. It concerned the rival claims of public campaigning and private life. She had already made various soundings concerning it, had had one or two preliminary interviews with dedicated campaigners of various sorts (including one with a man who, very much against Jemima's own beliefs, wanted to bring back capital punishment but whose wife opposed him). To her irritation, she was failing to turn up sufficient numbers of 'strong women' who fitted this particular bill; they existed all right, but preferred to keep their private lives and/or disputes to themselves. Jemima sympathised, of course, but remained professionally irritated . . .

Then Clemency Vane telephoned out of the blue. Jemima herself would certainly never have thought of a reformed (one hoped) drug dealer in connection with this series. Yet Clemency's original call, fielded by Cherry, indicated that this area of conflict was what she wished to discuss. Various other calls followed, guarded conversations, all on the telephone, with Jemima herself, with no direct information offered absolutely pertinent to the programme, yet a good deal of talk about the principles involved. Love and duty, their rival demands and so forth.

They had met only once; as now, in an hotel, an anonymous block in a different part of London; as now, the summons had come suddenly, giving Jemima little time to prepare.

'I can get away now,' Clemency Vane had said. 'Please come.' And Jemima, to the sound of a few protests about work load from Cherry, had gone.

For Clemency Vane's appearance, Jemima had been dependent on the numerous newspaper and television images from the time of her trial: the strong features, particularly the nose which might be described kindly as patrician, otherwise beaky; the circular tinted glasses which added a somewhat owlish look and the pretty softening halo of blonde curly hair at her trial. In fact Clemency was darker than Jemima had expected, or perhaps the blonde hair had been allowed to darken in prison; as it was, her hair, also much straighter, was scraped back, and her face behind the circular tinted glasses – they at least were familiar – was virtually devoid of make-up. You got the impression of someone deliberately rendering themselves unattractive or at least unappealing; gone was the feminine softness of the prisoner on trial.

At the same time Clemency was quite tiny physically; that, along with her cultivatedly plain appearance, was another surprise. Well, you never really knew about people from their newspaper photographs, did you? That was one certain rule. Even television could be oddly delusive about size and scale.

It was still a strong face, despite the unexpectedly small scale of it all. A strong face: and a strong character too, judging from the evidence yielded up by the trial.

'I need to find out about you,' Clemency had said at this meeting. She spoke quite abruptly, dragging on her cigarette. (She had smoked throughout the interview, stubbing out each cigarette with fury when it was about half-way finished.) 'I need to know if I can trust you.' Her attitude was certainly not conciliatory: defiant if anything. But she was also nervous.

'As it happens, you can trust me.' Jemima was prepared to be patient. 'But I hope you will find that for yourself. With time. That's the best way. I'm in no hurry about this series: we've only just started to research it, as a matter of fact. *For the Love of the Cause.* It's a fascinating topic but a tricky one. I need to get exactly the right people –'

'That piece in the paper – the woman spy in love with an Israeli – '

'Ah, you saw that. I wondered. Premature, I'm afraid. She won't talk to us. Too much conflict already about what she did for love.'

'I too did it for love.' Clemency interrupted her. 'You could say that I too gave up everything for love.' She was busy stubbing out yet another of those wretched cigarettes and she did not look at Jemima as she spoke.

'You mean there was a man involved?' Jemima spoke tentatively. Clemency's nervousness was not perhaps surprising under the circumstances but quite marked all the same, including this sudden out-of-the-blue request for a face-to-face interview. She had no wish to frighten her off at this stage.

'Correct. There was a man.' Clemency pulled on her cigarette with increasing ferocity and then once again stubbed it out.

'That didn't come out at the trial.'

'I didn't want it to. I pleaded "Guilty" and that was that.'

'Is he still involved? Or rather, are you still involved with him? You were in prison a long time. Or is it over? Is it this Love-versus-Duty question of the woman spy and the Israeli you mentioned? Is that what we might talk about on the programme?'

Jemima realised too late that she had posed too many questions too quickly. An obstinate closed expression on Clemency Vane's face warned her of her mistake.

'I don't want to say anything more at the moment. You must understand: there are problems.' And Clemency declined to explain any further, sharply and inexorably. That was all Jemima was left with – until the summons this morning.

So there was a man involved. And this was him? Was Jemima now looking at the man for whom Clemency, product of a privileged education, showered with worldly advantages by her doting parents, clever enough to achieve university, achieve anything she wished in truth, had thrown it all away? Infatuation was a fascinating subject. One woman's infatuation was another woman's poison . . . Take this man. Very strong physically perhaps (she hoped not to find out) certainly quite handsome . . . this was the man for whom a privileged English girl had wasted five years of her life. This Santangelino without even a name . . .

'My name is Alberto,' he said to her with a smile – his first smile, and that might be a good sign, might it not? Once again, however, he had apparently read her thoughts – not such a good sign, that.

'First of all you will take off all these clothes. Even the shoes now. Then we will know each other better. And perhaps we will love each other.' Alberto put both his big hands on her shoulders as though he was measuring her for something.

'Shouldn't we get to know each other first?' Jemima spoke in the most reasonable tone she could muster. She must at all costs, she knew from studying such things, humour him: she must not arouse his violence, his hostility, give him that psychological impetus he needed to transform the situation from polite parleying to physical action. It was the feeling of helplessness that was so terrible; just as she had been told so many times.

'And perhaps we will love each other.' For God's sake, it wasn't the stripping off that mattered! Jemima had a beautiful body, or at least had been assured of it enough times to lack self-consciousness on the subject. She had no particular feeling about nudity and privacy either, sunbathing topless or even naked when it seemed right without giving much thought to the subject. The exposure of her body, however disagreeable the demand in this secret claustrophobic context, was not the point. But to love each other!

How near, for example, was the hotel telephone? Looking round, she saw the telephone was on the far side of the bed. Her eye then fell on an ash-tray with stubs in it. That gave her an inspiration. It was worth a try: even for a dedicated non-smoker like herself.

'Could you let me have a cigarette first, please, then I promise –'

Alberto hesitated. Finally he said: 'I have no cigarettes.'

Jemima gazed again at the stubs. Half-smoked. In spite of herself, she found she was trembling. And her voice shook when she spoke. She had not realised before how much she had been counting – subconsciously – on Clemency's arrival to interrupt them, somehow save her. (Clemency Vane was after all the one person in the world who really did know where she was.)

Jemima looked at the bathroom door. It was closed. She had not really thought about it but now the blank door had a sinister look. 'What's happening here? Is she – wait a minute – is she *still* here? Is this a plot?'

Alberto smiled again. Jemima, her fear rising, decided that his smile was not after all a good sign.

'A plot? Yes, you could call it that,' he said. 'A plot to get to know you. You thought it was your plot with your silly programme about love and duty – even an intelligent woman like you, with your fine education, can be a little silly sometimes. But it was not your plot. It was our plot!'

'Clemency knows about this,' exclaimed Jemima. 'Well, she must. How else did you know I was coming? Listen, Clemency's here. That's what you're saying.'

'Don't you understand? Clemency would do anything for me. She's my woman. The drugs, everything, prison, that was all for me. And now she has brought you here for me. She set you up for me.'

'Clemmie told me to come here,' he went on with that strange horrible exhilaration. 'She laughed, yes, she laughed at you, for thinking that she would take part in your stupid programme.'

He was becoming vehement again and, apparently unaware of what he was doing, tightened the grip on her arm.

'I'm a strong man you see, the kind of man women love – women love to support and help men like me. Clemency knew that: strong man, she said, you get to know Jemima Shore then, if you want, get to know Jemima Shore if you like, because during all those years you never knew anything really about me. And now you never will. Poor Alberto, you will never know me.'

Alberto's grip had loosened again, and his voice too had changed subtly as though he was imitating Clemency herself. Her abrupt rather scornful tones. There was a silence between them.

'You will never know me.' But it was Alberto who had said that, quoting Clemency, not Jemima. It was Alberto himself imitating Clemency.

'She did do it all for me, didn't she?' He was questioning Jemima now; there was something pathetic about him, despite his fierceness, and the strong hands which still held her prisoner.

But then that temporary glimpse of something pathetic was quite gone. Alberto started to pull at Jemima's clothes. The cream-coloured jersey dress came off quite easily, or would have done so, but the very violence of his actions hindered him, those scrubbed strong hands seemingly frustrated by his own haste.

I must not struggle, thought Jemima desperately, I must not even scream. I know what to do, I must be passive, I must endure, I must survive. Otherwise he'll kill me. Now she was in her silk petticoat and the man was panting horribly, sweating much more. He began to talk, gabble: 'Women, you like this, this is what you really want, bitches, traitors . . . ' He talked on, and then half-hissed, half-shouted at her: 'You I'm really going to possess –'

In spite of herself Jemima lost control. The careful passivity went. She began to struggle in Alberto's grip, to shout at him.

'Even if you killed me,' having raped me was the unspoken phrase, for still, in spite of everything she did not wish to pronounce the words. 'Even if you killed me, and especially if you killed me, you would not get to know me. You would not possess me.'

Alberto stopped. He still held her. Now they were both sweating, panting.

'She said that, Clemency.' But before Alberto spoke the words, Jemima knew the truth, understood suddenly and clearly what had been implicit all the time. What had been done for love. Once long ago. And once only recently.

'Alberto,' she spoke more strongly now. 'Release me. Then let me go into the bathroom.'

'No. It's not right.' Some of the power was waning in him, the passion. Jemima felt it. Her own increased.

'She's there. Clemmie,' he added in a low voice.

'I – I want to see her,' said Jemima.

'There's nothing you can do.'

'You must let me go in there, there may be something I can do.'

Alberto shook his head. 'It's too late,' he said.

'Listen, for God's sake – '

'It's too late. It was already too late when you arrived here.' Now the force she had felt in him was totally extinguished. She was in command. In command as Clemency Vane had once been – had been until the very end.

'I followed her here,' he went on. 'I knew she was stealing out to come and see you. I pleaded with her when I got here. I knew she was trying to leave me, that she was getting frightened of what I might do to her. She found me so violent, so demanding after she came out of prison. She said sex didn't interest her. She never ever wanted to make love with me. She said I bored her.'

Alberto began to sob convulsively.

'Then when I pressed her more, she said she never loved me in the first place. She did it all for the cause. Yet I helped her. I protected her. She wouldn't listen. The money was needed then, she said, so she did what she had to do. Now it was not. Santangela was safe. And she would tell the world why she did it all – not for me, but for the country, the cause.'

He sobbed more terribly.

'For love.' Clemency's words came back to her. 'You could say indeed that I gave up everything for love.' Dry, wry, defiant words. But for love of the cause, not the man.

Jemima jumped up and Alberto did not even try to stop her. She pulled on her dress and he made no move to stop that either. She went into the little clean white hotel bathroom, saw the shower, the bright pristine towels on the rail, not very big towels and an unremarkable beige colour – it was that kind of hotel. All the towels were clean and untouched except one: that was the towel draped inadequately over the body of the woman lying in the bath.

The towel left her face exposed, or perhaps Alberto had not wished to cover it. Certainly he had not closed Clemency Vane's eyes: they stared at Jemima, sightless and bulging, above the purpled discoloration of her face, the mouth and the tongue. There was no sign of what Alberto had used to strangle her – but the memory of his strong, black-haired, well-tended, well-scrubbed-afterwards muscular hands came back to her. The hands which had held her, Jemima. And tried to know her, as in the end they had never known Clemency Vane.

'I told you it was too late,' Alberto said from the bedroom. He had not moved. 'You can go away now,' he added, in a remote voice as though the subject no longer interested him. 'I shan't harm you. Go. It's nothing to do with you any more.'

Much later, back at the Megalith office, Cherry said to Jemima with that cheerfulness she maintained even towards the end of the office day: 'Where were you this morning? There were quite a few calls. You left a message saying you were out seeing that woman, what's-her-name, the drug runner who did it all for love, the persistent one who kept ringing up about the new programme. But you never left me a number. Did you see her?'

'I saw her,' said Jemima. Later she would tell Cherry, of course, as she told her everything, and later still everyone would probably know. But not just now.

'Was there anything in it for the programme?' inquired Cherry. 'She was so sure she could help us.'

'No, after all, nothing in it for the programme.'

'Ah well,' said Cherry comfortably. 'You never really know about people, do you?'

Jemima Shore agreed.

BLOOD MATCH

Michael Gilbert

Last year, as students of the financial Press will remember, the old-established firm of Drake and Cowfold, linen-drapers and haberdashers (branches in North London and the Home Counties), 'went public'. That is to say, they published an advertisement which took up a whole page in *The Times* and the *Financial Times*, and contained a hotch-potch of unreadable information and incomprehensible figures, purporting to give the history of the firm from its beginnings as a draper's shop on Muswell Hill. Mr Rumbold, senior partner of Wragg & Rumbold, solicitors, of Coleman Street, was one of the few people who troubled to read the advertisement through from start to finish. He read it very carefully, taking off his glasses from time to time and polishing them with a linen handkerchief, and when he had finished reading, he smiled.

His firm had acted for the Cowfold family for nearly a century, and he had in front of him a statement, sworn by the late Lavinia Marcus-Cowfold, which gave a rather more detailed account of the rise of that respectable firm of linen-drapers and haberdashers. It was not only more detailed. It was a good deal more candid. It dealt with a number of instances of fraud, two of blackmail, two of theft, one of rape and one of murder.

Albert Drake and Hezekiah Cowfold had opened their first shop together in the year of Queen Victoria's Golden Jubilee. Both had considerable experience in this line, and both had made money. The shop which they opened was an ambitious one. In their advertisements they described it as 'The William Whiteleys of North London' and, if this was an exaggeration, the shop certainly was imposing, being full of shining brass and polished mahogany, and little metal containers which ran along on wire and gave a pleasant 'ting' as they arrived.

The partners were both typical Victorians, but were as different in outlook as two men could be. Hezekiah was a humanitarian. Albert was a buccaneer. To Hezekiah, shop assistants were souls to be saved. To Albert they were slaves. Differences of opinion were therefore bound to arise, and it is a tribute to their mutual tolerance that they got by as long as they did.

When the trouble came it was serious.

Hezekiah said, 'That little girl, the one they call Millie, on the glove counter, she's going to have a baby. She says it's yours.'

'Girls will say anything,' said Albert.

'She's going to say it in court.'

'What court, for God's sake?'

'The police court,' said Hezekiah. 'You realise she's only just fifteen now. If they believe her, you'll go to prison.'

'Has she been to the police yet?'

'Not yet.'

'I'll offer her five hundred pounds to keep her mouth shut. She'll take it.'

'She may take it,' said Hezekiah. 'I won't. The partnership's at an end. You can have your shares for what they cost you. Nothing more.'

Albert affected to consider the matter. Then he smiled and said, 'I dare say it's better that way. As a matter of fact, I've been thinking of retiring. I'm nearer sixty than fifty. We'll go to our lawyers and sort it all out tomorrow.'

Hezekiah was surprised. He had expected almost any other reaction. But then, Albert had often surprised him.

They both owned houses in Kent, and usually travelled home together. On this particular night there seemed to be no reason to vary their practise. They used the recently reopened Blackfriars overground station. It was a damp autumn night, with a thick mist rolling up from the river, and they strolled to the far end of the platform as they waited for the train.

When it arrived, Albert surprised Hezekiah for the last time by pushing him in front of it. No one saw him do it. The exposed end of the platform was very slippery. The coroner, recording a verdict of natural death, described it, with considerable accuracy, as 'a perfect death-trap'.

Wars are always good for linen-drapers. The South African war was no exception. By the time it had dragged to its close, and the boys had come home again, and married the girls they had left behind them, and trousseaus had been bought and houses had been furnished, Drake and Cowfold (now describing themselves as general suppliers) had opened branches in Hornsey and Crouch End, and Albert was beginning to feel that he could do with some help.

He selected as a second-in-command one of the returning heroes. This was Captain Toby Transome, a Cowfold cousin by marriage, who came back from the wars with a South African tan, a military moustache, and a DSO gained by the Captain, according to casual references he made to it, at the bloody skirmish of Elandslaagte. The Captain proved a good bargain. When the secretary of one of the leading West End Services Clubs came to discuss the bulk replacement of its table linen and cutlery, the deal went through noticeably more smoothly when he and the Captain discovered army acquaintances in common. Albert was so pleased that, three years later, he sold the Captain forty per cent of the shares in the company, carefully keeping sixty per cent, and control, in his own hands.

'When I die,' he used to say, with the cheerful unconcern of a man who has no intention of doing so in the foreseeable future, 'my shares will go to my son Maurice, and the firm will go from strength to strength under his chairmanship. And with your loyal help, my dear fellow,' he would add. Captain Transome used to smile.

Like all consistently healthy men, Albert died very suddenly. He collapsed at the celebrations which attended the opening of a new branch on Highgate Hill. Captain Transome summoned a doctor, and as soon as he was certain that Albert was indeed dead (no suggestion of foul play this time; a hot day, a heavy lunch and the excitement of the occasion was the doctor's accurate diagnosis) he hurried back to the headquarters of the company at Muswell Hill.

Here he went straight upstairs to the office, and told the secretary to summon the staff. As soon as he was alone in the room, he turned his attention to the safe in the corner. He had long possessed duplicates of Albert's more important keys, and it was the work of seconds to open the safe and the deed box inside it in which Albert kept his private papers. He inserted into this box a long, brown, legal-looking envelope which he had extracted from a locked drawer in his own desk. Then he relocked the box and safe and went down to break the news to the assembled staff.

It was at this point, Mr Rumbold remembered, that his firm had come into it. He recollected his father telling him about it. 'When they wound up Albert's estate,' he had said, 'one of the first things they did was to look through his private papers, and they found this envelope. It was an option agreement. Captain Transome was to have the option to acquire half of Albert's shares, at a proper valuation, after Albert's death. The copy among his papers was signed by Transome. *He* produced a duplicate copy, signed by Albert. The signature was a bit shakey, but not so shakey that anyone felt like standing up in court and suggesting it was a forgery. And anyway, there was the counterpart locked away in Albert's private box in his own safe. Maurice Drake kicked up a devil of a row. It meant that Transome had control of the company, and he would have to play second fiddle. However, he accepted it in the end, or appeared to do so. The business was booming, and there were plenty of profits for both of them.'

The corrupting effect of power has often been remarked on. Captain Transome was more corruptible than most. He married a widow from the shires, bought a town house in Hampstead and a hunting lodge in Leicestershire. His military past compensating, to a certain extent, for his commercial present, he was accepted by the more tolerant fringes of society and proceeded to enjoy to the full those last lush years of the Edwardian decade.

It was in 1911, during the blazing August of the Constitutional crisis, that a crisis of another sort developed at Drake and Cowfold. It was provoked by Maurice Drake.

He said to Captain Transome, who was paying one of his rare visits to the office, 'I'm afraid I've got rather an unpleasant job to do.'

'It's too hot for unpleasantness,' said the Captain, mopping his scarlet brow with a handkerchief. 'What is it? You got to sack someone?'

'In effect, yes,' said Maurice. 'I've got to sack you.'

This took some seconds to penetrate. When the Captain finally decided that Maurice was serious, he guffawed loudly and said, 'The heat's gone to your head, boyo. You can't sack me. I'm a majority shareholder. Actually, I could sack you.'

'But you're not going to,' said Maurice, 'and you're going to sell me enough of your shares to give me control.'

'Says who?'

'I say so.'

'And if I tell you to go to hell?'

'Then I shall publish the full and true facts of your career in South Africa. Such as, for instance, that you were not a captain but a very junior subaltern. That you took no part in the battle of Elandslaagte, or any battle for that matter, but spent the few months you actually were in South Africa looking after a supply dump in Cape Town.'

The Captain looked ugly. He said, 'No one's interested in the details of the South African war now.'

'The authorities would still be interested in the fact that you claimed a rank and a DSO to which you were not entitled.'

'Prove it.'

'Certainly. You had your photograph taken, in uniform, showing the badges of a rank you never reached, and the ribbon of a medal you never won.'

The Captain looked up sharply. The space on the wall which this photograph had occupied was empty. 'So you've pinched that old photograph, have you?' he said contemptuously. 'As far as I can remember, it's so faded you can hardly see a thing.'

'I was able to see one thing,' said Maurice. 'The name and address of the photographer who took it. I have a statement from him. He is prepared to produce his records in court, and say what you were wearing.'

There was a long silence. It seemed to be hotter than ever. Transome's face was now more puce than scarlet. He said, 'What do you want? What's the object of all this? It's a technical offence. The worst I could get would be a reprimand, or a fine.'

'You know damn well that wouldn't be all,' said Maurice. 'You'd have to resign from your club. No decent hunt would allow you out. You wouldn't be able to show your face in society. You might be able to put up with that – I don't know – but think what Marcia would say.' Transome thought about it. Marcia was his wife, a formidable woman with a tongue like the hunting crop she used so ruthlessly in the field.

'All right,' he said at last. 'What's your price?'

'Just enough shares to give me control,' said Maurice. 'and a reversion to the chairmanship when you go.'

Transome looked as though he was going to have a fit, but he managed to mutter 'I agree.' He did, in fact, have a stroke six months later, and died on Christmas Eve. In his certificate the doctor gave cirrhosis of the liver as the primary cause of death.

When the Germans invaded Belgium in 1914, and when patriotic crowds sang outside Buckingham Palace and young men rushed to an army which was far from ready to receive them, Maurice Drake kept his head. He decided that his talents would be more useful to England in the haberdashery and furnishing line than in the front line. 'After all,' as he pointed out to his chief cashier, 'anyone can be a soldier. But it takes years of skill and practice to judge between two linens or price a bedroom suite.' His chief cashier, who was ten years older than Maurice and suffered from a weakness in the lungs, said nothing at the time. Three months later, in the wet spring of 1915, he managed to get himself accepted for active service. He reached France in time to be a victim of the first gas attack, at Ypres. This did his lungs no good at all and he was dead before the end of the year.

Maurice accepted the loss philosophically. He promoted the second cashier. 'We shall all have to work a little bit harder,' he said. When, in 1917, the second cashier was called up too, Maurice very nearly went with him. He was well within the age for conscription. He managed, however, to persuade the local tribunal that the work he was then engaged on – he was specialising at the time in the production of army blankets and socks – was more important to the nation than the addition of one more infantry soldier to an army depleted by the Somme and preparing for Passchendaele. It was a narrow escape, however, and Maurice signified his gratitude by doubling his investment in the new War Loan.

After the Armistice, with business booming, it was clear that a major reorganisation of Drake and Cowfold was overdue. There were now eight branches in North London, and plans for opening three more in the Home Counties. The first side of the business which was going to need strengthening was the financial control. The second cashier, returned from Mesopotamia with a limp and the after-effects of amoebic dysentery, was quite unable to cope alone. He needed at least two assistants. But qualified accounts clerks cost money.

Maurice, casting his eye around the labour market, was one of the first to spot the potential of the newly emancipated woman worker. And it was agreeable both to his sense of economy and to his patriotism to offer a job, at a very modest wage, to a Mrs Marcus, a young war widow, whose husband, Commander Marcus, RN, had been killed at Jutland.

Mrs Marcus worked methodically and well, taking upon herself extra jobs which no one else wanted, writing up old ledgers, resuscitating forgotten accounts, sorting out the debris which five years of war had left in the cash department, and all for a tiny salary. After all, as Maurice reflected, she had her husband's pension to which he, as a super-tax payer, had contributed handsomely.

In the hard years of the middle and late twenties, with the General Strike and the unemployment which followed it, the economical Mrs Marcus proved invaluable to the company. And economies were necessary. Maurice sometimes used to wonder how on earth he could keep his two houses going. The town house in Kensington was not so difficult. It could be managed with a staff of three. But the country house at Leighton Buzzard, where his invalid wife spent most of her time, was a different proposition. Although reduced to the barest necessities, a companion and a personal maid for his wife, a cook, a man to drive the car and two gardeners, it still seemed to devour money. But what caused Maurice most distress was the iniquitous and ever-increasing burden of taxation. It seemed to him to be a sort of treachery that a Government which he supported willingly at election time with his vote should turn round on him later and try to rob him.

It was a fine summer morning in 1937, when England was beginning to shrug off the effects of the slump and the Stock Exchange index was slowly rising, that Mrs Marcus sought an interview with Maurice Drake.

She had been with the firm for seventeen years and, in her late thirties, combined natural good looks with the pose and composure of a woman who has made her own way. Maurice suspected that she had come to ask for a rise in salary and was prepared to offer her another fifty pounds a year. After all, she had been head cashier now for six years.

She came straight to the point. 'By my calculations,' she said, 'we have defrauded the Revenue, over the last six years, of something between forty-five and fifty thousand pounds. I imagine it went on before that but, since I wasn't head cashier then, I hadn't access to all the books.'

When Maurice was able to speak, he said, 'If anything of the sort has been going on – which I deny categorically – then it was the duty of the auditors to point it out to me.'

'Auditors are accountants, not detectives,' said Mrs Marcus. 'When invoices are concealed from them, when fictitious transactions are recorded between branches of the same firm, when certain cash receipts are entered only in a private ledger kept by you, and not produced to them at all . . . '

She continued for ten minutes giving chapter and verse with appalling fluency and detail.

'All right,' he said at last. 'All right, what's your price?' Even as he said it, he seemed to hear the echo of a voice all those years ago.

'I'm not looking for control,' said Mrs Marcus briefly. 'But I do think it's about time that a fifty per cent share came back into the Cowfold side, don't you?'

Seeing the look of surprise on Maurice's face, she laughed. 'You didn't know that my maiden name was Cowfold? Old Hezekiah was my grandfather. I've been interested in the doings of this firm for a long time – even before I joined it. I'd like the shares transferred into my full name, please – Lavinia Marcus-Cowfold. I intend, when I die, to leave them to my son. I have no doubt you will do the same with your shares. And talking of dying, I thought it wise – one never knows what accidents will occur – to leave a full account of the history of these transactions with my solicitor. To be opened at my death. Provided that it is *absolutely* clear that my death is due to natural causes, he has instructions not to publish anything.'

When Mr Rumbold had read the advertisement right through, he turned back again to the beginning, where the names of the Board of

Directors were set out. They included a Major-General, an ex-Lord Mayor and a peer of the realm. But, at the bottom of the list, he saw, in sinister proximity, the names of Michael Drake and Nicholas Marcus-Cowfold.

He had no idea who would be the final winner in that long drawn-out match, but he rather doubted whether it would be the company. He picked up his pen to finish a letter he was writing, in his own hand, to a client.

'I agree the prospects of this company look excellent,' he wrote. 'But I should not myself feel inclined to invest in it.'

THE HARD SELL

Catherine Aird

'Morning Harry.' Detective Inspector Sloan shifted his chair an inch or two to indicate to Inspector Harpe that there was room to sit beside him at the table in the police canteen.

'Morning.' The Inspector from Traffic set a mug of tea and a pile of ham sandwiches down on the table and pulled up a chair.

Sloan let him settle to food and drink before asking cautiously 'How's life?'

The caution was on account of Inspector Harpe's innate pessimism. He was known throughout the Berebury Division of the Calleshire Constabulary as Happy Harry because he had never been known to laugh. He on his part maintained that so far in Traffic there had never been anything at which even to smile.

'Busy,' he said, taking a bite.

This was not an unexpected reply since Inspector Harpe was head of 'F' Division's Traffic Department and thus never without work. In addition to this he maintained a ceaseless campaign against drinking and driving – and an even more bitter one against those lawyers and magistrates whose view of what constituted random breath-testing did not coincide with his own.

Detective Inspector Sloan, who was himself head of the tiny Criminal Investigation Department of Berebury Division, let the tea and sandwiches exert their customary beneficial effect on Harpe's temper before venturing further comment.

'All well in your neck of the woods?' he enquired presently. 'Like the motorway?' After drinking-drivers Inspector Harpe reserved his ferocity for fast ones and was in the habit of referring to Calleshire's short stretch of motorway as the Route of All Evil.

Happy Harry grunted. 'Had a fatal last night.'

Sloan nodded sympathetically. This, no doubt, accounted for some of his colleague's taciturnity. Road traffic accidents, however trivial, were never exactly fun and where there was a death involved they were even less nice and, no matter what anyone said, policemen never did get inured to them. He said, 'There's always too many RTA's . . .'

'This wasn't exactly a road traffic accident.' Harry frowned. 'At least not within the meaning of the Act.'

'How come that you got it then?' asked Detective Inspector Sloan professionally curious.

'The caller said there'd been a car accident and so naturally we attended.'

'And had there?'

'Oh, yes, there had been a car accident, all right,' responded Harpe simply, 'and it was certainly death by motor car. I'll grant you that.'

'I wonder how the statisticians will deal with it, then,' mused Sloan. He'd never felt the same way about statisticians since he'd heard about the one who had drowned in a river whose average depth was six inches . . .

'It's not the numbers game that I'm interested in,' snorted Harpe.

Sloan toyed with the idea of repeating the old joke about statisticians to Happy Harry but decided against it. Instead he asked, 'What happened then?'

'Funniest thing,' said Harpe. 'It was at this meeting of the Calleshire Classic Car Club. They have their get-togethers at . . .'

'I know,' said Sloan. 'Down at the old railway goods yard.'

'More's the pity,' said Harpe: this was another beef of the Traffic Inspector's. 'Now if all the freight went by goods waggon on the railways we'd have half the traffic and a quarter of the problems we get on the roads.'

'And if all the population stuck to the Ten Commandments,' said the head of 'F' Division's Criminal Investigation Department, 'then I'd be out of a job. What happened, Harry?'

'Well, you know the goods yard as well as I do. They've still got some old platforms down there even though they've taken up the tracks as well as the waste ground where the old railway sidings used to be . . .'

'Berebury North Station,' supplied Sloan. 'That was.'

'Closed by the good Dr Beeching, I suppose . . .'

'No,' said Sloan, who was Calleshire born and bred. 'Berebury North closed before the war when the fish trade fell away. The herring failed. What happened yesterday?'

'Well, they were using the old railway down platform to show off these classic cars. They don't make them like that any more, Sloan. Beautiful jobs, they are. You should have seen the old Aston Martin they had there. Now there's a car with everything . . .'

'What happened?'

But there was no rushing the Traffic man: he might have been making a statement to the court, his tale was so measured. 'They'd just got the cars all lined up in a row with their front wheels right up to the edge of the platform so that they could have their photographs taken for some magazine. Lovely to see proper bodywork and real chrome . . .'

'Best side to London if it was the down platform,' observed Sloan.

Irony was always wasted on Inspector Harpe who paused, searching for a good simile. 'Like so many race horses.'

'Were they showing their paces too?' enquired Sloan, 'and pawing the ground?'

'There's no need to be sarcastic, Sloan. They all go – it's just that they don't go far or so fast these days.'

'No different really then from any other geriatrics, eh?' Sloan took a drink from his own cup. 'And do I take it, Harry, that one of them went far enough to kill someone?'

The Traffic Inspector nodded, his mouth full of sandwich. 'Sort of,' he mumbled.

'While it was on the down platform?'

The nod was even more vigorous this time.

'It went over the platform?' divined Sloan.

'That's right.' The sandwich had gone down the red lane now. 'A pearl-grey 1961 2.4 Jaguar came off over the edge and fell on to a chap who was thinking of buying it.' A rare flash of humour burgeoned over Happy Harry's melancholy features. 'He bought it all right.'

'Who was at the wheel?'

'Didn't I say, Sloan? That was the interesting thing. No one.'

'No one?'

'As many witnesses as any court could want are ready and willing to swear to there having been no one – but no one – in the car when it moved forward. First thing they looked at . . . after sending for us and the ambulance, of course.'

'What about the engine?'

'Ticking over in drive. You see, the owner – a man by the name of Daniel White – was trying to persuade the deceased to take the Jaguar in settlement of some betting debt and was making him listen to how sweet the engine sounded when it took this great leap forward like the Chinese under Mao Tse-tung.'

'Did the throttle-return spring snap?' suggested Sloan whose interest in foreign affairs wasn't as far-reaching as it should have been. His grandfather had always worried about the Yellow Peril: he was more interested in a newly killed man. 'Metal fatigue must be a problem in those old things.'

'First thing we checked after we'd got the body out from under,' grunted Harpe. 'Right as ninepence – the throttle-return spring, I mean. Ned Molland was dead.'

'I see.'

'Mind you, he must have been just in front of the Jag at the time it hit him and a good three feet below it . . .'

'Why?'

'White said he wanted Molland to stand there to hear the engine running – if he could.'

'Why shouldn't he have heard it?' asked Sloan. 'Was he deaf or something?'

Inspector Harpe looked disappointed. 'Don't you remember that old ad about the Rolls-Royce clock being the only thing you could hear when the engine was running or something?'

'Harry, I'm not a motor man and I'm not an advertising man, just a plain old-fashioned policeman, detective branch. 'What about the brakes?'

'I think,' said Inspector Harpe judiciously, 'you could say that the brakes were half on.'

'Or half off,' observed Detective Inspector Sloan detachedly.

'Not that that should have made all that difference,' said Harpe. 'According to an independent witness – the owner of the next car along – an old Armstrong Siddeley – paintwork still black as night – they built cars to last in those days, Sloan . . .'

'The witness . . .' Sloan reminded him. He, himself, was never prepared to describe any witness, sight unseen, as independent, but then, as he would have been the first to admit, he was in the detective branch.

'The witness said that the engine of the Jaguar had been running for quite a little while before the car moved forward apparently all on its own.'

'Odd,' agreed Sloan thoughtfully.

'Apparently Ned Molland . . .'

'The victim,' said Sloan. There was, after all, no doubt about that.

'Him,' said Harpe ungrammatically. 'Apparently he hadn't been all that keen on taking the car in the first place. He'd already got an old Lanchester, you see, and anyway the car was worth more than what White owed him.'

'So there would've been a balance payable?'

'Seems as if that was one of the things that was putting Ned Molland off buying,' said Harpe, who had obviously been pretty diligent in his way. 'All White'll get now, of course, will be the insurance money.'

'And his debt rubbed out,' murmured Sloan reflectively, 'if it was a gaming one.'

'Must say I hadn't thought of that,' admitted Harpe.

'Brake cable didn't fail?' asked Sloan, though he knew Happy Harry would have checked on that too.

'No.' Harpe frowned.

'Why did White leave the engine ticking over and the gear shift in drive?' asked Sloan. 'Sounds dangerous to me.'

'Oh, you can do that with an automatic. No problem.'

'Well, there was this time from the sound of it. Why did he do it anyway?'

'Like I said, I think he just wanted to impress on Ned Molland how quiet the engine was.'

'And instead,' remarked Sloan, 'he seems to have impressed the engine on him, poor fellow. Well, Harry, put me out of my misery. If it wasn't the brakes, what was it then? Mice?'

'I don't think it was mice, Sloan,' said Inspector Harpe seriously. 'I think it was just old age and bad luck.'

'What was?'

'The hose connecting the manifold to the brake servo splitting just when it did. It's rubber and I should say that it was pretty badly perished to start with.' Harry drained his tea and said lugubriously, 'Only to be expected in a car of that date, of course, though there was a patch of oil on it too and that always accelerates perishing. All it needed was the vibration from the engine running for a bit to fracture it completely.'

'Then what?' Sloan held up a hand: 'But spare me too many technicalities, Harry.'

'When that hose breaks you lose your vacuum,' said Happy Harry simply.

'And we all know that Nature abhors a vacuum,' said Sloan patiently. 'So what happens next?'

'You get a sudden inrush of air into the manifold.'

'And?' said Sloan, draining his cup.

'And that would cause the engine to speed up momentarily.'

'Would it, indeed?' said Sloan thoughtfully.

'And that,' continued Harpe, 'would bring the torque converter into operation.'

'So?'

'So the car would leap forward before the engine died.'

'The creditor it was who died,' murmured Sloan almost to himself.

'I reckon that White was dead lucky not to have got killed, too,' said Inspector Harpe. 'If he hadn't been standing where he was, to one side, he would have been. More tea?'

'Thanks,' replied Sloan abstractedly. 'Harry, what about the rest of the engine? Did you find anything wrong at all?'

'Not a thing. I went over the inside, too.' He sighed. 'I checked the dashboard. Lovely piece of work . . .'

'What is?' said Sloan, his mind elsewhere.

'The dashboard. Polished walnut. You don't see that sort of thing any more these days.' He sighed again. 'I'd quite forgotten how good real leather smells.' Inspector Harpe got to his feet. 'Another round of sandwiches, too? Ham, wasn't it?'

'No, thanks. Just the tea.' Sloan sat and stared unseeingly round the police canteen, his mind elsewhere, until Inspector Harpe came back.

'One tea, no sugar, coming up . . .'

'Harry, that was no accident last night.'

'What?' said Harry, lowering his cup without drinking anything. 'Sloan, are you saying that . . .'

'I am suggesting that the car might have a lovely smell but that the accident has a very nasty one.' He leaned forward. 'Listen, Harry, suppose this man Daniel White created just the right degree of perishing in the vacuum pipe himself and knew that the vibration caused by letting the engine run for a little while would mean that sooner or later it would be bound to fracture . . .'

'Having carefully placed his victim in front of and slightly below the car before it shot forward,' contributed the Traffic man intelligently.

Sloan nodded. You could say this for old Harry: he wasn't slow to cotton on. 'And having set things up so that he wasn't in the car himself . . .'

'Neat, I call it,' said Harpe appreciatively.

'All White had to do,' said Sloan, 'was to stand well back himself and he's in the clear in both senses. How to lose a creditor and collect on the insurance in – er – one fell swoop.' He drained his tea. 'I'd say you were dealing with murder, Harry.'

'Oh, no, I'm not,' said Inspector Harpe vigorously. 'You are, Sloan. It's not my Department. I'm Traffic, remember?'

THE CORDER FIGURE

Peter Lovesey

Mrs D'Abernon frowned at the ornamental figure on the shelf above her. She leaned towards it to read the name inscribed in copperplate on the base.

'Who was William Corder?'

'A notorious murderer.'

'How horrid!' She sheered away as if the figure were alive and about to make a grab at her throat. She was in the back room of Francis Buttery's second-hand bookshop, where cheap sherry was dispensed to regular buyers of the more expensive books. As a collector of first editions of romantic novels of the twenties and thirties, she was always welcome. 'Fancy anyone wanting to make a porcelain effigy of a murderer!'

'White earthenware,' Buttery told her as if that were the only point worth taking up. 'Staffordshire. I took it over with the shop after the previous owner passed on. He specialised in criminology.' He picked it up, a glazed standing figure about ten inches in height.

'The workmanship looks crude to me,' ventured Mrs D'Abernon, determined not to like it. 'I mean, it doesn't compare with a Dresden shepherdess, does it? Look at the way the face is painted; those daubs of colour on the cheeks. You can see why they needed to write the name on the base. I ask you, Mr Buttery, it could be anyone from the Prince of Wales to a peasant, now, couldn't it?'

'Staffordshire portrait figures are not valued as good likenesses,' Buttery said in its defence, pitching his voice at a level audible to browsers in the main part of the shop. He believed that a bookshop should be a haven of culture, and when he wasn't broadcasting it himself, he played Bach on the stereo. 'The proportions are wrong and the finishing is too stylised to admit much individuality. They are primitive pieces, but they have a certain naive charm, I must insist.'

'Insist as much as you like, darling,' said Mrs D'Abernon, indomitable in her aesthetic judgements. 'You won't convince me that it is anything but grotesque.' She smiled fleetingly. 'Well, I might give you vulgar if you press me, as I'm sure you'd like to.'

Buttery sighed and offered more sherry. These sprightly married women in their thirties and forties who liked to throw in the occasional suggestive remark were a type he recognised, but hadn't learned how to handle. He was thirty-four, a bachelor, serious-minded, good-looking, gaunt, dark, with a few silver signs of maturity at the temples. He was knowledgeable about women – indeed, he had two shelf-lengths devoted to the subject, high up and close to the back room, where he could keep an eye on anyone who inspected them – but he had somehow failed to achieve what the manuals described as an intimate relationship. He was not discouraged, however; for him, the future always beckoned invitingly. 'The point about Staffordshire figures,' he persisted with Mrs D'Abernon, 'is that they give us an insight into the amusements of our Victorian ancestors.'

'Amusements such as murder?' said Mrs D'Abernon with a peal of laughter. She was still a pretty woman with blonde hair in loose curls that bobbed when she moved her head.

'Yes, indeed!' Buttery assured her. 'The blood-curdling story of a man like Corder was pure theatre, the stuff of melodrama. The arrest, the trial and even the execution. Murderers were hanged in public, and thousands came to watch, not just the rabble, but literary people like Dickens and Thackeray.'

'How macabre!'

Buttery gave the shrug of a man who understands human behaviour. 'That was the custom. Anyway, the Staffordshire potters made a tidy profit out of it. I suppose respectable Victorian gentlemen felt rather high-hat and manly with a line of convicted murderers on the mantelpiece. Of course, there were other subjects, like royalty and the theatre. Sport, as well. You collected whatever took your fancy.'

'And what did Mr William Corder do to earn his place on the mantelpiece?'

'He was a scoundrel in every way. No woman was safe with him, by all accounts,' said Buttery, trying not to sound envious. 'It happened in 1827, way out in the country in some remote village in Suffolk. He was twenty-one when he got a young lady by the name of Maria Marten into trouble.'

Mrs D'Abernon clicked her tongue as she took a sidelong glance at the figure.

'The child didn't survive,' Buttery went on, 'but Corder was persuaded to marry Maria. It was a clandestine arrangement. Maria dressed in the clothes of a man and crossed the fields with Corder to a barn with a red roof, where her luggage was stored and a gig was supposed to be waiting to take them to Ipswich. She was not seen alive again. Corder reappeared two days after, and bluffed it out for months that Maria was living in Ipswich. Then he left the district and wrote to say that they were on the Isle of Wight.'

'And was he believed?' asked Mrs D'Abernon.

'By everyone except one tenacious woman,' said Buttery. 'That was the feature of the case that made it exceptional. Mrs Marten, Maria's mother, had two vivid dreams that her daughter had been murdered and buried in the red barn.'

'Ah! The intrusion of the supernatural,' said Mrs D'Abernon in some excitement. 'And did they find the poor girl there?'

'No one believed Mrs Marten at first, not even her husband, but, yes, eventually they found Maria buried under the floor. It was known as the Red Barn Murder, and the whole nation was gripped by the story. Corder was arrested and duly went to the gallows.' He paused for effect, then added, 'I happen to have two good studies of the case in fine condition, if you are interested.'

Mrs D'Abernon gave him a pained look. 'Thank you, but I don't care for that sort of reading. Tell me, what is it worth?'

'The figure of Corder? I've no idea.'

'It's an antique, isn't it? You ought to get it valued.'

'It's probably worth a few pounds, but I don't know that I'd care to sell it,' said Buttery, piqued that she had dismissed the books so off-handedly.

'You might, if you knew how much you could get for it,' Mrs D'Abernon remarked with a penetrating look. 'I'll make some inquiries. I have a very dear friend in the trade.'

He would have said, 'Don't trouble,' but he knew there was no stopping her. She was a forceful personality.

And next afternoon, she was back. 'You're going to be grateful to me, Mr Buttery,' she confidently informed him as he poured the sherry. 'I asked my friend and it appears that Staffordshire figures are collectors' items.'

'I knew that,' Buttery mildly pointed out.

'But you didn't know that the murderers are among the most sought after, did you? Heaven knows why, but people try to collect them all, regardless of their horrid crimes. Some of them are relatively easy to obtain if you have a hundred pounds or so to spare, but I'm pleased to inform you that your William Corder is extremely rare. Very few copies are known to exist.'

'Are you sure of this, Mrs D'Abernon?'

'Mr Buttery, my friend is in the antique trade. She showed me books and catalogues. There are two great collections of Staffordshire figures in this country, one at the Victoria and Albert Museum and the other owned by the National Trust, at Stapleford Park. Neither of them has a Corder.'

Buttery felt his face getting warm. 'So my figure could be valuable.' He pitched his voice lower. 'Did your friend put a price on it?'

'She said you ought to get it valued by one of the big auctioneers in London and she would be surprised if their estimate was lower than a thousand pounds.'

'Good gracious!'

Mrs D'Abernon beamed. 'I thought that would take your breath away.'

'A thousand!' said Buttery. 'I had no idea.'

'These days, a thousand doesn't go far, but it's better than nothing, isn't it?' she said as if Buttery were one of her neighbours on Kingston Hill with acres of grounds and a heated swimming pool. 'You might get more, of course. If you put it up for auction, and you had the V and A bidding against the National Trust . . .'

'Good Lord!' said Buttery. 'I'm most obliged to you for this information, Mrs D'Abernon.'

'Don't feel under any obligation whatsoever, Mr Buttery,' she said, flashing a benevolent smile. 'After all the hospitality you've shown me in my visits to the shop, I wouldn't even suggest a lunch at the Italian restaurant to celebrate our discovery.'

'I say that *is* an idea!' Buttery enthused, then, lowering his voice again, 'That is, if your husband wouldn't object.'

Mrs D'Abernon leaned towards Buttery and said confidentially, 'I wouldn't tell him, darling.'

Buttery squirmed in his chair, made uneasy by her closeness. 'Suppose someone saw us? I'm pretty well known in the High Street.'

'You're probably right,' said Mrs D'Abernon, going into reverse. 'I must have had too much sherry to be talking like this. Let's forget it.'

'On the contrary, I shall make a point of remembering it,' Buttery assured her, sensing just in time that the coveted opportunity of a liaison was in danger of slipping by. 'If I find myself richer by a thousand pounds, I'll find some way of thanking you, Mrs D'Abernon, believe me.'

On Wednesday, he asked his part-time assistant, James, to manage the shop for the day. He got up earlier than usual, packed the Corder figure in a shoe box lined with tissue, and caught one of the commuter trains to London. In his corduroy jacket and bow-tie he felt mercifully remote from the dark-suited businessmen ranged opposite him, most of them doggedly studying the city news. He pictured Mrs D'Abernon's husband reading the same paper in the back of a chauffeur-driven limousine, his mind stuffed with stock market prices, uninterested in the dull, domestic routine he imagined his wife was following. Long might he remain uninterested!

The expert almost cooed with delight when Buttery unwrapped his figure. It was the first William Corder he had ever seen, and a particularly well-preserved piece. He explained to Buttery that Staffordshire figures were cast in simple plaster moulds, some of which were good for up to two hundred figures, while others deteriorated after as few as twenty castings. He doubted whether there were more than three or four Corders remaining in existence, and the only ones he knew about were in America.

Buttery's mouth was dry with excitement. 'What sort of price would you put on it?' he asked.

'I could sell it today for eight hundred,' the expert told him. 'I think in an auction it might fetch considerably more.'

'A thousand?'

'If it went in one of our sales of English pottery, I would suggest that figure as a reserve, sir.'

'So it might go for more?'

'That is my estimation.'

'When is the next sale?'

The expert explained the timetable for cataloguing and pre-sale publicity. Buttery wasn't happy at the prospect of waiting several months for a sale, and he inquired whether there was any way of expediting the procedure. With some reluctance, the expert made a phone call and arranged for the Corder figure to be added as a late item to the sale scheduled the following month, five weeks ahead.

Two days later, Mrs D'Abernon called at the shop and listened to Buttery's account of his day in London. She had sprayed herself lavishly with a distinctive floral perfume that subdued even the smell of the books. She appeared more alluring each time he saw her. Was it his imagination that she dressed to please him?

'I'm thrilled for you,' she said.

'And I'm profoundly grateful to you, Mrs D'Abernon,' said Buttery, ready to make the suggestion he had been rehearsing ever since he got back from London. 'In fact, I was wondering if you would care to join me for lunch next Wednesday as a mark of my thanks.'

Mrs D'Abernon raised her finely plucked eyebrows. 'I thought we had dismissed the possibility.'

'I thought we might meet in Epsom, where neither of us is so well known.'

She gave him a glimpse of her beautiful teeth. 'How intriguing!'

'You'll come?'

She put down her sherry glass. 'But I think it would be assuming too much at this stage, don't you?'

Buttery reddened, 'How, exactly?'

'One shouldn't take anything for granted, Mr Buttery. Let's wait until after the sale. When did you say it is?'

'On May the fifteenth, a Friday.'

'The fifteenth? Oh, what a pity! I shall be leaving for France the following day. I go to France every spring, before everyone else is on holiday. It's so much quieter.'

'How long will you be away?' Buttery asked, unable to conceal his disappointment.

'About a month. My husband is a duffer as a cook. He can survive for four weeks on rubbery eggs and burnt bacon, but that's his limit.'

Buttery's eyes widened. The future that had beckoned ever since he had started to shave was now practically tugging him by the sleeve. 'You go to France without your husband?'

'Yes, we always have separate holidays. He's a golfer, and you know what they're like. He takes his three weeks in July and plays every day. He doesn't care for travel at all. In fact, I sometimes wonder what we *do* have in common. Do you like foreign travel, Mr Buttery?'

'Immensely,' said Buttery huskily, 'but I've never had much opportunity . . . until this year.'

She traced the rim of the sherry glass with one beautifully manicured finger. 'Your thousand pounds?'

'Well, yes.' He hesitated, taking a glance through the shop to check that no one could overhear. 'I was thinking of a trip to France myself, but I don't know the country at all. I'm not sure where to head for.'

'It depends what you have in mind,' said Mrs D'Abernon, taking a sip of the sherry and giving Buttery a speculative look. 'Personally, I adore historical places, so I shall start with a few days in Orléans and then make my way slowly along the Loire Valley.'

'You can recommend that?'

'Absolutely.'

'Then perhaps I'll do the same. I say,' he added, as if the idea had just entered his head, 'wouldn't it be fun to meet somewhere in France and have that celebration meal?'

She registered surprise like a star of the silent screen. 'Yes, but you won't be going at the same time as I . . . will you?'

Buttery allowed the ghost of a smile to materialise fleetingly on his lips. 'It could be arranged.'

'But what about the shop?'

'Young James is perfectly capable of looking after things for me.' He topped up her glass, sensing that it was up to the man to take the initiative in matters as delicate as this. 'Let's make a rendezvous on the steps of Orléans Cathedral at noon on May the eighteenth.'

'My word, Mr Buttery! . . . Why May the eighteenth?'

'So that we can drink a toast to William Corder. It's the anniversary of the Red Barn Murder. I've been reading up on the case.'

Mrs D'Abernon laughed. 'You and your murderer!' There was a worrying pause while she considered her response. 'All right, May the eighteenth it is – provided, of course, that the figure is sold.'

'I'll be there whatever the outcome of the sale,' Buttery rashly promised her.

Encouragingly, she leaned forward and kissed him lightly on the lips. 'So shall I.'

When she had gone, he went to his Physiology and Anatomy shelf and selected a number of helpful volumes to study in the back room. He didn't want his inexperience to show on May the eighteenth.

The weeks leading up to the auction seemed insufferably long to Buttery, particularly as Mrs D'Abernon appeared in the shop only on two occasions, when by sheer bad luck he happened to be entertaining other lady customers in the back room. He wished there had been time to explain that it was all in the nature of public relations, but on each occasion Mrs D'Abernon curtly declined his invitation to join the sherry party, excusing herself by saying she had so many things to arrange before she went to France. For days, he agonised over whether to call at her house – a big detached place overlooking the golf course – and eventually decided against it. Apologies and explanations on the doorstep didn't accord with the cosmopolitan image he intended to present in Orléans.

So he made his own travel arrangements, such as they were: the purchase of an advance ticket for the cross-Channel ferry, some travellers' cheques and a map of the French railway system. Over there, he would travel by train. He gathered that Mrs D'Abernon rented a car for her sight-seeing, and that would have to do for both of them after Orléans, because he had never learned to drive. He didn't book accommodation in advance, preferring to keep his arrangements flexible.

He also invested in some new clothes for the first time in years: several striped shirts and cravats, a navy blazer and two pairs of white, well-cut trousers. He bought a modern suitcase and packed it ready for departure on the morning after the auction.

On May the fifteenth, he attended the auction. He had already been sent a catalogue, and the Corder figure was one of the final lots on the list, but he was there from the beginning, studying the form, spotting the six or seven dealers who between them seemed to account for three-quarters of the bids. They made him apprehensive after what he had once read about rings that conspired to keep the prices low, and he was even more disturbed to find that a number of items had to be withdrawn after failing to reach their reserve prices.

As the auction proceeded, Buttery felt increasingly nervous. This wasn't just the Corder figure that was under the hammer; it was his rendezvous with Mrs D'Abernon, his initiation into fleshly pleasures. He had waited all his adult life for the opportunity, and it couldn't be managed on a low budget. She was a rich, sophisticated woman, who would expect to be treated to the best food and wines available.

'And so we come to Lot 287, a very fine Staffordshire figure of the murderer, William Corder . . .'

A pulse throbbed in Buttery's head and he thought for a moment he would have to leave the sale room. He took deeper breaths and closed his eyes.

The bidding got under way, moving rapidly from five hundred pounds to seven hundred and fifty pounds. Buttery opened his eyes and saw that two of the dealers were making bids on the nod at an encouraging rate.

'Eight hundred,' said the auctioneer.

There was a pause. The bidding had lost its momentum.

'At eight hundred pounds,' said the auctioneer. 'Any more?'

Buttery leaned forward anxiously. One of the dealers indicated that he had finished. This could be disastrous. Eight hundred pounds was below the reserve. Perhaps they had overvalued the figure.

'Eight-fifty on my left,' said the auctioneer, and Buttery sat back and breathed more evenly. Another dealer had entered the bidding. Could he be buying for the V and A?

It moved on, but more slowly, as if both dealers baulked at a four-figure bid. Then it came.

'One thousand pounds.'

Buttery had a vision of Mrs D'Abernon naked as a nymph, sipping champagne in a hotel bedroom.

The bidding continued to twelve hundred and fifty pounds.

The auctioneer looked around the room. 'At twelve hundred and fifty pounds. Any more?' He raised the gavel and brought it down. 'Hudson and Black.'

And that was it. After the auctioneers' commission had been deducted, Buttery's cheque amounted to eleven hundred and twenty-five pounds.

Three days later, in his blazer and white trousers, he waited at the rendezvous. Mrs D'Abernon arrived twenty minutes late, radiant in a primrose yellow dress and wide-brimmed straw hat, and pressed her lips to Buttery's, there on the cathedral steps. He handed her the box containing an orchid that he had bought in Orléans that morning. It was clearly a good investment.

'So romantic! And two little safety-pins!' she squeaked in her excitement. 'Darling, how thoughtful. Why don't you help me pin it on?'

'I reserved a table at the Hôtel de la Ville,' he told her as he fumbled with the safety-pin.

'How extravagant!'

'It's my way of saying thank you. The Corder figure sold for over a thousand pounds.'

'Wonderful!'

They had a long lunch on the hotel terrace. He ordered champagne and the food was superb. 'You couldn't have pleased me more,' said Mrs D'Abernon. 'To be treated like this is an almost unknown pleasure for me, Mr Buttery.'

He smiled.

'I mean it,' she insisted. 'I don't mean to complain about my life. I am not unloved. But this is another thing. This is romance.'

'With undertones of wickedness,' commented Buttery.

She frowned. 'What do you mean?'

'We're here by courtesy of William Corder.'

Her smile returned. 'Your murderer. I was meaning to ask you: why did he kill poor Maria?'

'Oh, I think he felt he was trapped into marriage,' Buttery explained. 'He was a philanderer by nature. Not a nice man at all.'

'I admire restraint in a man,' said Mrs D'Abernon.

'But, of course,' Buttery responded, with what he judged to be the ironic smile of a man who knows what really pleases a woman.

It was after three when, light-headed and laughing, they stepped through the hotel foyer and into the sunny street.

'Let's look at some shops,' Mrs D'Abernon suggested.

One of the first they came to was a jeweller's. 'Aren't they geniuses at displaying things?' she said. 'I mean, there's so little to see in a way, but everything looks exquisite. That gold chain, for instance. So elegant to look at, but you can be sure if I tried it on, it wouldn't look half so lovely.'

'I'm sure it would,' said Buttery.

'No, you're mistaken.'

'Let's go in and see, then. Try it on, and I'll give you my opinion.'

They went in and, after some rapid mental arithmetic, Buttery parted with three thousand francs to convince her that he really had meant what he said.

'You shouldn't have done it, you wicked man!' she told him, pressing the chain possessively against her throat. 'It was only a meal you promised me. I can't think why you did it.'

Buttery decided to leave her in suspense. Meanwhile, he suggested a walk by the river. They made their way slowly down the rue Royale to the Quai Cypierre. In a quiet position with a view of the river, they found a *salon de thé*, and sipped lemon tea until the shadows lengthened.

'It's been a blissful day,' said Mrs D'Abernon.

'It hasn't finished yet,' said Buttery.

'It has for me, darling.'

He smiled. 'You're joking. I'm taking you out to dinner tonight.'

'I couldn't possibly manage dinner after the lunch we had.'

'Call it supper, then. We'll eat late, like the French.'

She shook her head. 'I'm going to get an early night.'

He produced his knowing smile. 'That's not a bad idea. I'll get the bill.'

Outside, he suggested taking a taxi and asked where she was staying.

She answered vaguely, 'Somewhere in the centre of town. Put me off at the cathedral, and I can walk it from there. How about you? Where have you put up?'

'Nowhere yet,' he told her as he waved down a cab. 'My luggage is at the railway station.'

'Hadn't you better get booked in somewhere?'

He gave a quick, nervous laugh. She wasn't making this easy for him. 'I was hoping it wouldn't be necessary.' The moment he had spoken, he sensed that his opportunity had gone. He should have sounded more masculine and assertive. A woman like Mrs D'Abernon didn't want a feeble appeal to her generosity. She wanted a man who knew what he wanted and took the initiative.

The taxi had drawn up and the door was open. Mrs D'Abernon climbed in. She looked surprised when Buttery didn't take the seat beside her.

He announced, 'I'm taking you to lunch again tomorrow.'

'That would be very agreeable, but –'

'I'll be on the cathedral steps at noon. Sweet dreams.' He closed the door and strode away, feeling that he had retrieved his pride and cleared the way for a better show the next day. After all, he had waited all his life, so one more night in solitary was not of much account.

So it was a more assertive Buttery who arrived five minutes late for the rendezvous next day, found her already waiting and kissed her firmly on the mouth. 'We're going to a slightly more exotic place today,' he told her, taking a decisive grip on her arm.

It was an Algerian restaurant on the fringe of the red light district. Halfway through their meal, a belly dancer came through a bead curtain and gyrated to taped music. Buttery clapped to the rhythm. At the end, he tossed the girl a five-franc piece and ordered another bottle of wine.

Towards three o'clock Mrs D'Abernon began to look restless.

'Had enough?' asked Buttery.

'Yes. It was wonderfully exciting and I enjoyed every minute of it, but I have to be going. I really must get back to my hotel and wash my hair. It must be reeking of cigar smoke and I made an appointment for a massage and manicure at five.'

'I'll give you a massage,' Buttery informed her with a no-nonsense statement of intention that pleased him as he said it. It more than made up for the previous day's ineptness.

'That won't be necessary, thank you,' responded Mrs D'Abernon, matching him in firmness. 'She's a qualified masseuse and beautician. I shall probably have a facial as well.'

He gaped at her. 'How long will that take?'

'I'm in no hurry. That's the joy of a holiday, isn't it?'

Buttery might have said that it was not the joy he had in mind, but he was too disconcerted to answer.

'We could meet again tomorrow for lunch, if you like,' offered Mrs D'Abernon.

He said, letting his resentment show, 'Do you really want to?'

She smiled benignly. 'Darling, I can think of nothing I would rather do.'

That, Buttery increasingly understood, was his problem. Mrs D'Abernon liked being treated to lunch, but there was nothing she would rather do. Each day that week she made some excuse to leave him as soon as possible afterwards: a hair appointment, a toothache, uncomfortable shoes. She declined all invitations to dinner and all suggestions of night-clubbing or theatre-visiting.

Buttery considered his position. He was going through his travellers' cheques at an alarming rate. He was staying at a modest hotel near the station, but he would have to pay the bill some time, and it was mounting up, because he spent each evening drinking alone in the bar. The lunches were costing him more than he had budgeted and there was nearly always a taxi fare to settle.

In the circumstances, most men planning what Buttery had come to France to achieve would have got discouraged, cut their losses, and given up, but Buttery was unlike most other men. He still nursed the hope that his luck would change. He spent many lonely hours trying to work out a more successful strategy. Finally, desperation and his dwindling funds drove him to formulate an all-or-nothing plan.

It was a Friday, and they had lunch at the best fish restaurant in Orléans, lobster scooped wriggling from a tank in the centre of the dining room and cooked to perfection, accompanied by a vintage champagne. Then lemon sorbet and black coffee. Before Mrs D'Abernon had a chance to make her latest unconvincing excuse, Buttery said, 'I'd better get you back to your hotel.'

She blinked in surprise.

'I'm moving on tomorrow,' Buttery explained. 'Must get my travel arrangements sorted out before the end of the afternoon.' He beckoned to the waiter.

'Where do you plan to visit next?' asked Mrs D'Abernon.

'Haven't really decided,' he said as he settled the bill. 'Nothing to keep me in Orléans.'

'I was thinking of driving to Tours,' Mrs D'Abernon quickly mentioned. 'The food is said to be outstanding there. I could offer you a lift in my car if you wish.'

'The food isn't so important to me,' said Buttery.

'It's also very convenient for the châteaux of the Loire.'

'I'll think it over,' he told her, as they left the restaurant. He hailed a taxi and one drew up immediately. He opened the door and she got in. 'Hôtel Charlemagne,' he told the driver as he closed the door on Mrs D'Abernon. He noticed her head turn at the name of the hotel. It hadn't been difficult to trace. There weren't many that offered a massage and beauty service.

She wound down the window. 'But how will I know . . .?' Her words were lost as the taxi pulled away.

Buttery gave a satisfied smile as he watched her go.

He went to the florist's and came out with a large bouquet of red roses. Then he returned to his hotel and took a shower.

About seven, he phoned the Hôtel Charlemagne and asked to speak to Mrs D'Abernon.

Her voice came through. 'Yes?'

In a passable imitation of a Frenchman, Buttery asked, 'You are English? There is some mistake. Which room is this, please?'

'Six-five-seven.'

He replaced the phone, went downstairs to the bar and ordered his first vodka and tonic.

Two hours later, carrying the roses, he crossed the foyer of the Charlemagne and took the lift to the sixth floor. The corridor was deserted. He found 657 and knocked, pressing the bouquet against the spy-hole.

There was a delay, during which he could hear sounds inside. The door opened a fraction. Buttery pushed it firmly and went in.

Mrs D'Abernon gave a squeak of alarm. She was dressed in one of the white bathrobes that the best hotels provide for their guests. She had her hair wrapped in a towel and her face was liberally coated in a white cream.

'These are for you,' said Buttery in a slightly slurred yet, he confidently believed, sexy voice.

She took the roses and looked at them as if a summons had been served on her. 'Mr Buttery! I was getting ready for bed.'

'Good,' said Buttery, closing the door. He crossed to the fridge and took out a half-bottle of champagne. 'Let's have a nightcap.'

'No! I think you'd better leave my room at once.'

Buttery moved closer to her, smiling. 'I don't object to a little cream on your face. It's all right with me.' He snatched the towel from her head. The colour of her hair surprised him. It was brown, and grey in places, like his own. She must have been wearing a blonde wig all the times he had taken her to lunch.

Mrs D'Abernon reacted badly. She flung the roses back at him and said, 'Get out of here!'

He was not discouraged. 'You don't mean that, my dear,' he told her. 'You really want me to stay.'

She shook her head emphatically.

Buttery went on, 'We've had good times together, you and I. Expensive lunches.'

'I enjoyed the lunches,' conceded Mrs D'Abernon, in a more conciliatory vein. 'Didn't I always express my appreciation?'

'You said you felt romantic.'

'I did, and I meant it!'

'Well, then.' He reached to embrace her, but she backed away. 'What's the matter with you? Or is something the matter with me?'

'No. Don't think me unappreciative, but that's enough for me, to have an escort during the day. I like to spend my evenings alone.'

'Come on, I've treated you well. I've spent a small fortune on you.'

'I'm not to be bought,' said Mrs D'Abernon, edging away from the bed.

'It's not like that at all,' Buttery insisted. 'I fancy you, and I reckon you fancy me.'

She gave an exasperated sigh. 'For pity's sake, Mr Buttery, I'm a married woman. I'm used to being fancied, as you put it. I'm sick of it, if you want to know. All evening he ignores me, then he gets into bed and thinks he can switch me on like the electric blanket. Coupling, that's all it is, and I want a break from it. I don't want more of it. I just crave a little innocent romance, someone to pay me some attention over lunch.' Then Mrs D'Abernon made her fatal mistake. She said, 'Don't spoil it now. This isn't in your nature. I picked you out because you're safe. Any woman could tell you're safe to be with.'

Safe to be with? He winced, as if she had struck him, but the effect was worse than that. She had just robbed him of his dream, his virility, his future. He would never have the confidence now to approach a woman again. He was finished before he had ever begun. He hated her for it. He hated her for going through his money, cynically eating and spending her way through the money he had got for his Corder figure.

He grabbed her by the throat.

Three days later, he returned to England. The French papers were full of what they described as the Charlemagne killing. The police wished to interview a man, believed to be English, who had been seen with the victim in several Orléans restaurants. He was described as middle-aged, going grey, about 5 ft 8 ins and wearing a blue blazer and white trousers.

In Buttery's well-informed opinion, that description was worse than useless. He was 5 ft 9 ins in his socks, there was no grey hair that anyone would notice and thirty-four was a long way from being middle-aged. Only the blazer and trousers were correct, and he had dumped them in the Loire after buying jeans and a T-shirt. He felt amused at the problems now faced by all the middle-aged Englishmen in blue blazers staying at the Charlemagne.

He experienced a profound sense of relief at setting foot on British soil again at Dover, but it was short-lived, because the immigration officer asked him to step into an office and answer some questions. A CID officer was waiting there.

'Just routine, sir. Would you mind telling me where you stayed in France?'

'Various places,' answered Buttery. 'I was moving along the Loire Valley. Angers, Tours, Poitiers.'

'Orléans?'

'No. I was told it's a disappointment historically. So much bombing in the war.'

'You heard about the murder there, I expect?'

'Vaguely. I can't read much in French.'

'An Englishwoman was strangled in her hotel bedroom,' the CID man explained. 'She happens to come from the same town as you.'

Buttery made an appropriate show of interest. 'Really? What was her name?'

'Mildred D'Abernon. You didn't meet her at any stage on your travels?'

He shook his head. 'D'Abernon. I've never heard of her.'

'You're quite sure?'

'Positive.'

'In that case, I won't detain you any longer, Mr Buttery. Thank you for your co-operation.'

In the train home, he tried to assess the case from the point of view of the police. In France, there was little, if anything, to connect him with the murder. He had travelled separately from Mrs D'Abernon and stayed in different hotels. They had met for lunch, but never more than once in the same restaurant and it was obvious that the descriptions provided by waiters and others could have applied to hundreds, if not thousands, of Englishmen. He had paid every bill in cash, so there was no question of his being traced through the travellers' cheques. The roses he had bought came from an old woman so short-sighted that she had tried to give the change to another customer. He had been careful to leave no fingerprints in the hotel room. The unremarkable fact that he came from the same Surrey suburb as Mrs D'Abernon and had been in France at the same time was hardly evidence of guilt.

All he had to do was stay cool and give nothing else away.

So he was irritated, but not unduly alarmed, when he was met off the train by a local policeman in plain clothes and escorted to a car.

'Just checking details, sir,' the officer explained. 'We'll give you a lift back to your place and save you the price of a taxi. You live over your bookshop, don't you?'

'Well, yes.'

'You answered some questions at Dover about the murder in Orléans. I believe you said you didn't know Mrs D'Abernon.'

'That's true.'

'Never met the lady?'

Buttery sensed a trap. 'I certainly didn't know her by name. Plenty of people come into the shop.'

'That clears it up then, sir. We found a number of books in her house that her husband understands had been bought from you. Do you keep any record of your customers?'

'Only if they pay by cheque,' said Buttery with a silent prayer of thanks that Mrs D'Abernon had always paid in cash.

'You don't mind if I come in, then, just to have a glance at the accounts?'

The car drew up outside the shop and the officer helped Buttery with his cases.

It was after closing time, but James was still there. Buttery nodded to him and walked on briskly to the back room, followed by the policeman.

'Nice holiday, Mr Buttery?' James called. 'The mail is on your desk. I opened it, as you instructed.'

Buttery closed the door, and took the account book off its shelf. 'If I'd had any dealings with the woman, I'm sure I'd remember her name,' he said, as he held it out.

The officer didn't take it. He was looking at an open parcel on Buttery's desk. It was about the size of a shoe box. 'Looks as if someone's sent you a present, sir.'

Buttery glanced into the box and saw the Corder figure lying in a bed of tissue paper. He picked it out, baffled. There was a letter with it from Hudson and Black, dealers in *objets d'art*. It said that the client they had represented in the recent auction had left instructions on the day of the sale that the figure of William Corder should be returned as a gift to its seller with the enclosed note.

The policeman picked out a small card from the wrappings, frowned at it, stared at Buttery and handed it across.

Buttery went white. The message was handwritten. It read:
You treated me to romance in a spirit of true generosity. Don't think badly of me for devising this way to show my gratitude. I can well afford it.

It was signed: *Mildred D'Abernon.*

Below was written: *P.S. Here's your murderer.*

THE MOUSE WILL PLAY

Margaret Yorke

Mrs Bellew surveyed her neighbours through the large picture window of her living room at number 17 Windsor Crescent. Across the road, the fair young man with the beard was getting into his Sierra, briefcase already placed in the rear. Two small children and their mother watched him leave, all waving. Up and down the street, other morning rituals were taking place. Some husbands sprang into their cars and drove away without a visible farewell; at several houses both partners – you could not be certain they were married nowadays – left home daily. Soon the Crescent would settle into its weekly mode as the children left for school, the younger ones with their mothers, others alone, a few in groups. Then the toddlers would come out to play – a few, to Mrs Bellew's horror, in the street. Mrs Bellew's own son had never played in the street.

She was, as far as she could tell, the only senior resident on the estate, and she had been accustomed to a very different life.

Mrs Bellew's husband had died a year ago, suddenly, of a heart attack while in Singapore on business. Until then, hers had been a busy, fulfilling existence, acting as his hostess as his own business expanded. Frequently, guests who were in fact his customers were entertained at Springhill Lodge to dinner, or even for an entire weekend, with a round of golf or a swim in the Bellews' kidney-shaped azure pool. Deals were mooted and concluded around the Bellews' mahogany dining-table while Mrs Bellew and the visiting wife chatted of this and that in the drawing room and the hired Cordon Bleu cook cleared up in the kitchen. Mrs Bellew planned the menus but never prepared them.

Occasionally, in her turn, Mrs Bellew travelled abroad with Sam and was, herself, entertained, but not on that last journey.

And now it had ended, with Sam heavily in debt.

After his death their son had decided that his mother must be resettled in a small, easy-to-manage house on a bus route and within walking distance of a general store, for she would not be able to afford a car. Thus it was that she had been uprooted from her large house with its two acres of garden in Surrey and despatched to this commuter village where she knew no one.

She could catch the train to London easily, her son had pointed out, to visit him and her grandchildren, and it was not far from his own weekend cottage in the Cotswolds.

Mrs Bellew would have agreed that the distance was not great if she could have been whisked there in Sam's Rover, or even in her own Polo, but there was no way of getting to Fettingham from Windsor Crescent by public transport without two changes of bus involving a long wait between them, so she stayed away. Giles had said he would often fetch her for a visit, and this had happened once, but Mrs Bellew had not enjoyed the weekend spent in the damp stone cottage which Giles and his wife were renovating. While they spent their time decorating or in the pub, Mrs Bellew was expected to mind the children and to cook the lunch. Chilled and miserable, Mrs Bellew was thankful to return to 17 Windsor Crescent, with its central heating.

But her days were long and solitary. She kept to a routine of housework, as she had done throughout her life before she had anyone to help her with it, but she could not dust and polish all day. Meals were dull. She missed not Sam so much as what went with him – the bustle of his life and its purpose, as well as the comforts she had now grown used to, which his money bought; and she felt bitter anger at his failure to leave her properly provided for. Now she was no one, just an elderly woman living in a modern house – one of the smaller on the estate – among other anonymous houses in an area where there was no sense of community. Mrs Bellew did not require the services of Meals on Wheels or the old people's day centre. It did not occur to her that she could have usefully lent her aid and experience to either of these organisations.

When Sam died, the deal that he had been negotiating had been intended to put his business back in profit, but meanwhile his credit was extended, funds borrowed and despatched, like Antonio's argosies, to earn reward, and like those, some were lost. He had pledged his main insurance on this last project.

'You've got to face it, Mother. Father was a speculator and his gamble came unstuck,' Giles had told her sternly. 'If he hadn't died, he'd have been in serious trouble.' It had taken all Giles's own considerable ingenuity to rescue what he had from the collapse of his father's ventures, and he had been unable to spare his mother the discovery that the old man had died as he had lived, dangerously, in bed with a young Chinese woman.

Now, nothing broke the monotony of Mrs Bellew's days. No Sam, red-faced and cheerful, returned with tales of successfully concluded deals.

How many of such stories had been lies? Like his protests that he missed her when he went abroad?

These thoughts were unendurable. Mrs Bellew would not entertain them and instead she concentrated on her neighbours. Which of them, superficially so self-satisfied and smug, with their rising incomes and, in many cases, their second car and salary, were living lies?

Wondering about them, Mrs Bellew began to notice things. There was the dark blue Audi which left number 32 each morning at half-past seven and was sometimes absent for several days at a time. One day she saw the owner, a man in his late thirties, carrying an overnight bag to the car. Like Sam's, his job obviously involved travel. She watched the house while he was gone and saw a green Porsche parked outside it until very late at night. Mrs Bellew soon identified the driver, a young man with fair curly hair.

The cat's away, she thought, and that mouse is playing.

She noticed other things: an impatient, angry mother cuffing her small son about the head as they walked along the road bound for the nursery school; older children on roller skates who swung on trees that overhung the pavement, breaking branches and skating off, giggling, before they were discovered. She began to keep a record, writing down the habits of her neighbours in a notebook. She knew no one's name, but within the compass of her vision from her window she observed which wife was visited by her mother every Tuesday; who was called on by a man in a Triumph Spitfire every Wednesday afternoon; who cleaned and polished – such women were seen in pinafores cleaning windows – and who employed someone to help them. She recognised her neighbours in the supermarket in the local town and saw how they laid out their money: who bought frozen food in bulk; who spent vast sums on pet food; who was frugal. Walking along the street on winter afternoons, she could see through the large lighted windows into rooms where women spent hours eating chocolates and watching television.

Some of them had secrets and she began to learn them.

Mrs Bellew prepared the letters carefully, cutting the words from a magazine and pasting them on to plain sheets of Basildon Bond. She planned every operation with the same meticulousness that had made her dinner parties so successful, choosing each victim when she was confident of her facts, and finding out their names from the voters' list.

She wrote to the social security office about the child she saw cuffed in the street, and soon had the satisfaction of seeing an official-looking woman calling at the house. Later, the child's mother went away. The window-cleaner – almost her only contact apart from the postman and the milkman – told her that the father, left alone with the child and a job to do, could not cope and the small boy had been taken into care.

'A shame, I call it,' said the window-cleaner. 'Been knocking the kid about, it seems – the mother had. Girls don't know they're born, these days. But I don't know – poor little lad. It makes you think.'

Mrs Bellew agreed that indeed it did. She was surprised at the outcome of her intervention; still, the boy would be looked after now.

She did not fear discovery; the recipients of her letters would not broadcast their own guilt. On trips to London, which were cheap because she used her old person's rail card though she did not like to think that she looked old, Mrs Bellew mailed her serpent missives. Then she would indulge herself in tea at Harrods before catching her train home. She would prepare the next offensive whilst awaiting the outcome of the last.

One Wednesday, the husband of the woman visited by the Triumph Spitfire driver came home unexpectedly. He caught his wife *in flagrante* with the young man from the estate agent's who had sold the house to them, and went straight round to see the young man's wife who had also been ignorant of what was going on. Eventually, both couples separated. Four school-age children were involved, two in each family.

Mrs Bellew soon had the interest of watching new neighbours move into number 25.

The window-cleaner expressed dismay that there had been so much unhappiness on the estate lately. He'd heard that Mrs Fisher's mother, who came to see her daughter every Tuesday, had been asked by her son-in-law to restrict her visits because it was time Mary Fisher pulled herself together and stood on her own feet after her fourth miscarriage. She ought to get a job, her husband had told her, and stop brooding. She'd told the window-cleaner all about it when he went round and found her weeping bitterly.

Mrs Bellew was surprised to hear about the miscarriages. Her letter to Mr Fisher had mentioned his wife's child-like dependency on her mother and suggested she was idle. To the window-cleaner, she opined that sitting about indulging in self-pity was not constructive.

Mrs Bellew went on a summer visit to her son and his family in their cottage. This began as a better experience than the last; she sat in a deckchair for an hour reading *Good Housekeeping*, but was expected to cook the Sunday lunch while her son and his wife met their friends, fellow weekenders, in the local pub. The children were delighted as their grandmother had been left a leg of lamb to roast; on other Sundays a precooked pie, bought from the local butcher, was their lot. It was a grandmother's pleasure to cherish her family, Giles's wife stated firmly; her own mother liked nothing better than to cook for any number.

'Get her to do it, then,' said Mrs Bellew, demanding to be taken home early.

She was in time to see an ambulance drawn up outside the Fishers' house, but she did not learn what had happened until the next visit of the window-cleaner. He told her without any prompting.

Mrs Fisher had tried to kill herself. She had swallowed various pills, drunk a lot of sherry, and gone to bed with a plastic bag over her head. Woozy with the sherry and the drugs, she had used a bag already perforated for safety and so she had survived, though she was deeply unconscious when discovered by her next-door neighbour. Mary's mother had known that Tim Fisher, an enthusiastic golfer, was playing a double round that day. Unable to reach her daughter on the telephone, she called the neighbour. Tim had come back from the golf course grumbling about neurotic women.

There was a satisfactory amount of coming and going to please Mrs Bellew for several days after this. She knew that Tim Fisher would never show her original letter to a soul, and she did not make the mistake of following it with a second. She had a new target lined up in her sights now.

In the local supermarket, she had noticed the woman from number 43 buying gin and sherry – such a lot of it, several bottles every week. The woman's face was flushed; she was one of those who watched television in the afternoons.

Neatly and painstakingly, Mrs Bellew cut the words from *Homes and Gardens*. The paper was pleasanter to work with than ordinary newsprint, which made one's fingers inky.

Does your wife take her empty gin bottles to the bottle bank? Mrs Bellew inquired, in careful composition. Her messages were always terse, just enough to sow disquiet.

Dick Pearson showed his wife the letter when he tackled her. There were tears and recriminations as Barbara confessed to feeling useless and lonely while the children, both now teenagers, were at school all day. Dick didn't want her to go to work; his was an income adequate for their needs and a mother's place was in the home; besides, she had no proper qualifications.

Now he felt shame. Busy chasing orders for his firm, which dealt in manufacturing equipment, he had failed to think of her, even to talk to her when he was at home. But for the anonymous letter, he was thinking, she could have ended up like Mary Fisher.

Had there been a letter there?

He could not ask, but both he and Barbara wondered.

Mary Fisher left the hospital at last. When she came home, her mother resumed her visits, and Barbara Pearson, trying to redeem herself, also took to calling round. The two women began to discuss launching a joint enterprise, catering for private parties – even, perhaps, business lunches in the local town. Both were skilful cooks.

The idea burgeoned. They had cards printed and put notices in the local paper. Then they distributed leaflets.

'That woman at number 17,' said Barbara. 'She always looks so elegant, but she must be getting on. I wouldn't mind betting she'd appreciate a bit of help when she entertains. And she might have well-off friends who'd use us, too. Let's go and see her.'

Mary, wrapped in her own misery, had barely noticed Mrs Bellew. She thought she looked stuck-up.

She went to call, with Barbara.

Mrs Bellew, unaccustomed, now, to company, recognised them both and at first she did not want to let them in. But Barbara said they needed her advice, and so, reluctantly, she admitted them.

In her elegant living room, Barbara described their plan.

Mrs Bellew said she never entertained now, but had done a lot during her husband's lifetime. She waxed eloquent about *milles feuilles* and Chicken Supreme.

'You should join us,' Barbara enthused. 'Your experience would be invaluable.'

Six months ago, Mrs Bellew might have considered it; she knew all about well chosen, balanced menus. But now she was already wondering how she could bring them down, for she had learned to hate success.

Mary had problems concentrating these days. Her attention wandered, and she picked up a magazine from the coffee table in front of her, leafing idly through it. Mrs Bellew saw what she was doing, rose swiftly and removed the magazine from her grasp as if she was a child touching a forbidden object. Without a word of explanation, she put it in a drawer and soon the interview had ended.

'Wasn't that odd of her?' said Mary as they left. 'But it was rude of me, I suppose, to look at it when we were meant to be talking. Sorry.'

'She was ruder,' Barbara said.

'There were holes in it,' said Mary.

'Holes?'

'Sort of like windows. Pieces cut from different pages.'

'Recipes cut out?'

'No. Bits in the middle of a story,' Mary said.

Barbara had seen the letter sent to Dick. He alone of all the recipients in Windsor Crescent had shown it to its subject.

Next Friday, Mrs Bellew went, as usual, to the supermarket in the local town. Barbara was also there. She had often seen the older woman buying one packet of butter, her small portion of frozen food, and had vaguely pitied her. Now, she was curious; she'd thought a lot about the mutilated magazine. Whoever had written that letter to Dick had either seen her buying drink or disposing of her empties and so was local, though the letter had had a London postmark. So many small tragedies had happened lately in the area; other people might have been receiving letters too.

Watching Mrs Bellew study prices on some chops, Barbara selected two pairs of tights she did not want. She scarcely thought about it as she passed behind Mrs Bellew who was stooping forward, peering into the freezer chest, her wicker basket gaping on her arm. Barbara, not even worrying in case she was observed herself, dropped the tights into it and moved on.

They might not be discovered. Nothing might be done about it if they were, especially if Mrs Bellew proclaimed her ignorance of how they got there.

Far off among the cereals, Barbara missed the small commotion at the door as Mrs Bellew was led away for questioning.

POISONED TONGUES

Susan Moody

Martin Fensome was already a household name when he bought the cottage next door to mine. With two successful novels behind him and his third being touted as one of the hottest literary properties of the year, he was, at thirty-two, well on the way to becoming the kind of major crime writer that I, ten years older and only two books further on, could never hope to be.

Not that I particularly envied him. Fame often seems to me to have been achieved at the expense of compassion. Martin, particularly, appeared to have trouble accommodating the weaknesses of others, despite his apparent understanding of the often pathetic characters who peopled his pages. Perhaps I gave him too much credit; it is possible that the understanding I thought I glimpsed was in fact merely a prop to illustrate more clearly his invariable theme of an eye for an eye. Nor did he make any attempt to hide his steely determination to succeed in his chosen field by whatever means he had at his command. It is a trait that many writers lack; those that possess it usually try to hide it since it often gives rise to a sneering hostility among their peers.

'Why crime?' I asked him once.

'Why not?' He grinned at me with conscious charm. He smiled in exactly the same way from the back of his book covers.

I shrugged. 'Crime writers have such a hard time establishing any literary credibility. It's taken people like Rendell and le Carré years to be seen as good writers rather than as writers of good crime fiction.'

'True.' He rubbed his face thoughtfully. 'I wonder if it would make you a better crime writer if you had personal knowledge of what it's like to commit a crime.'

'It would be bound to, provided you had the ability to start with. You'd be writing out of real knowledge, real feeling, then.'

'Ability doesn't have much to do with it. Look at you, for instance. Let's face it, your books are infinitely better written and crafted than mine are. Yet . . .'

'I'm not particularly well-known, you mean?'

'Yes.' He sat by my fire, his face darkly sardonic. 'You can't be naive enough to think that we writers achieve status on merit alone.'

'Actually, I rather think I am,' I said.

He laughed. 'You've got to put yourself about more. Make contacts. Get yourself talked about. Show them who you are.'

'Difficult, when I'm not awfully sure of that myself.'

Nor was I awfully sure who Martin was. Yet, in spite of our different personalities, we became friends of a sort. I had thought I had him pinned down, dissected and filed away, the separate pieces of him ready to be brought out and used to give veracity to a fictional character next time I needed them. It was Nathalie Benson who made me realise that I might have been wrong in my assessment of him.

Nathalie was the daughter of the couple who lived in Lantern House on the edge of the village. He was something big in banking; she was American. Nathalie had been sent to her mother's old college – Vassar, if I remember rightly – after finishing her education in England, and consequently did not meet Martin for a good eighteen months after his arrival among us.

She was a striking girl, tall and willowy, with one of those pale pretty faces that are usually referred to as pre-Raphaelite, and a quantity of reddish-fair hair. She was working for BBC Radio and had plenty of the kind of transatlantic polish that appeals to men like Martin.

I confess I had not believed him capable of falling so passionately in love. But fall he did. So much so that he, the intolerant dissector of the flaws in others, was blind to those in her. Had I realised how total his commitment to Nathalie was to become, I might even have tried to warn him. Or maybe I would not have done: once set on their paths, I have found that people seldom alter their course, however explicit the danger signs. And what, after all, was there for me to warn him of? The time she overdosed on sleeping-pills in her first year at college? She always maintained it was not a suicide attempt, merely the result of stress and fatigue. Or the time she crashed her father's car into a tree in broad daylight on a straight piece of road? Another accident, she claimed, something to do with hitting the wrong pedal with her foot. It was established by the police that she had not been drinking and the fact that she had just been thrown over by her boyfriend was not mentioned. At least, not officially, though the village gossips – particularly Maggie Underwood, Jean Wallace and Laura Pettifer – made sure the rest of us knew.

Anyway, trying to talk to Martin of neurosis would have been pointless. 'What kind of neurosis?' he would have quite rightly asked. 'What do you mean?'

And of course I meant little beyond my awareness in Nathalie of something faintly unstable, a recognition that the roots of her personality were too shallowly planted. Nothing I could have put my finger on, pointed to, said: 'Here, Martin, is the danger that could cause you pain in the future.'

The whole village was invited to the wedding. The only absentees were Maggie Underwood, and the Wallaces. Kenneth and Jean Wallace pretended to be desolated at missing the big occasion, though we all knew that they had only arranged their holiday in Rhodes after the invitations had been sent out. And Maggie discovered that she had to be in London that day, something to do with sorting out the General's memoirs. None of us mentioned, even to each other, that Jean had crossed swords with Martin more than once over the way he parked his car on the village green, and that Maggie had been rudely rebuffed by him when she called about the Conservative fête. I confess I was surprised to see Laura Pettifer there, in view of the fact that Martin had once called her an interfering old bat to her face: she came with Tim, her much-doted-on son, who was in his first year as a trainee accountant and destined, so Laura said, to be a high-flyer in the City.

The occasion passed off smoothly, despite the faint curl of the groom's mouth as he greeted the local guests, and the somewhat overly dramatic way the bride sobbed her way into the car taking them to the airport as though she was never going to return. They were to fly off to Japan for three weeks; I had no doubt that some of the trip would figure in Martin's next tax return as an allowable expense. Laura Pettifer made a point of crossing the road the following day to ask me if I'd noticed the way Martin had been pawing the bridesmaids but I said sharply that she must have been imagining it, managing to imply that she had perhaps imbibed rather more champagne than she should have. That annoyed her and she departed with huffy shoulders.

Naturally, I did not call next door without an invitation, once the newly-weds returned from their honeymoon. I saw little of Martin over the next few months; Nathalie did not care for me much, nor I for her. In between the bouts of working at my next book, I began to realise just how much I missed Martin's acerbic conversation and outrageous cynicism, but respect for a writer's working hours kept me away, despite the fact that Nathalie changed jobs and began to travel up to London every day and even stayed overnight from time to time.

Then he invited me to dinner. 'You've got to meet this friend of mine,' he said. 'He's in television. Could do you a bit of good.'

Guy Henderson looked as if he had done a lot of people a bit of good in his time, most of them women. He also looked as if the good he'd done had mainly been for his own benefit. But perhaps I just don't go for that brand of looks: big body, beard, hungry blue eyes set in one of those enthusiastic red faces under a lot of springing blondish hair.

It seemed fairly obvious that Nathalie, on the other hand, did. However much I reminded myself that she and Guy Henderson were in the same line of business and would naturally have a lot in common, their rapport seemed both instantaneous and exaggerated. He was down here, doing a programme for one of those literary slots the BBC like to put out from time to time: *Bookends*, or something like that, I believe it was called. It was to follow a typical working month in the life of one of our leading young novelists: Martin Fensome. Henderson seemed totally uninterested when Martin introduced me as a fellow-writer. Over the next few months, so he assured the table, though his eyes were on Nathalie, we would be seeing a lot of him. Naturally I did not say that I would be fairly content to see nothing of him at all.

It was not very long after this that the rumours started. I think I first heard it from Jean Wallace, at one of the monthly Parish Council meetings.

'Saw them together in London, at L'Escargot,' she said, over a cup of instant coffee. 'Sitting awfully close together!' She smiled in the coyly innocent way that was her speciality, and none of us even thought to wonder what she herself was doing in so up-market a restaurant.

Laura Pettifer was next. 'His car,' she said. 'Parked in a lay-by when I was picking Tim up from his grandparents.'

'And they were both inside?' I asked.

'Well, I couldn't actually see them,' she admitted. 'But Tim thought he saw Nathalie's scarf draped over the back of the passenger seat. And why else would Guy's car be there?'

'Why else?' What did she mean? I am often stunned by the vicious priggishness that is stirred by the thought of other peoples' sexuality, especially in the supposedly virtuous. I pointed out that Guy Henderson was here to make a film: he could well have been looking for a specific location. I waxed quite lyrical over the Young British Novelist striding across the fields seeking inspiration from Nature, followed by the BBC cameras, but they were unconvinced.

Then Maggie Underwood had a go. Maggie came to the village a determined spinster some twenty-five years ago, and has remained determined ever since. Partly, I think, from want of opportunity to be otherwise. But also because a husband would have detracted from her own importance as the undoubted leader of local society. Her position in the village was unassailable: she was the daughter of General Underwood who had been something high-powered in India, and she occupied herself chiefly with editing his memoirs and drinking tea with those of her neighbours she considered well-bred enough to handle her bone-china teacups.

'They were holding hands,' she said, in her thin well-bred voice. 'I saw them.' She allowed a faint smear of distaste to crease her carefully powdered face.

'Where?' asked Laura, greedily . . .

Maggie put down the disposable plastic cup which is all the vicar sees fit to provide us with at our meetings. 'Oh, my dear, the train!'

'A bit indiscreet, isn't it?' said Jean. 'I mean, you never know who'll be coming down from London.'

'But that's not all,' Maggie declared. 'I saw them coming out of the Station Hotel first.'

'They were probably having a drink before the train,' I said.

'Hand in hand?'

'They're in show biz,' I said. 'People like that are always much more demonstrative than the rest of us.'

What I said cut absolutely no ice with them. They were convinced that Nathalie and Guy were having a full-fledged affair.

Naturally, when Nathalie announced a few months later that she was expecting a baby in the summer, there were a lot of significant looks round the village.

'Oh yes?' sneered Laura Pettifer in the village shop. 'I wonder who the father is.'

'Poor Martin,' was Jean Wallace's contribution, along with a sorrowful shake of her head.

And Maggie Underwood, who had literary pretensions, thanks to the General's memoirs, made some remark about cuckolds that I am glad to say I did not quite catch.

Who told Nathalie? Difficult to say. By the time she was beginning to show, the whole village knew of the theory that the child-to-be's father was not Martin but Guy. Suffice it to say that somehow she found out.

I should really have warned Martin, I suppose. But he was so proud of his wife, longing so intensely for the baby, that I found myself quite incapable of saying anything to him that would spoil his delight in either.

Then I woke up one night to discover my bedroom full of flashing blue lights. Looking out, I saw an ambulance outside Martin's gate, and men carrying a stretcher into the house.

I put on a dressing-gown and went next door. Martin was distraught. 'It's Nathalie,' he said.

'A miscarriage?'

'No.' He watched as the ambulance men backed down the steep cottage stairway with a stretcher. 'She tried to hang herself.'

'What?'

'Yes. From the beam in the bedroom. Luckily the rope broke. She must have hit the floor f-frightfully hard. There was b-blood everywhere.'

His chin wobbled painfully. Martin, the cynic, the wit, the analyser of other peoples' tragedies, was having trouble with his own. Even as I tried to comfort him, I found myself wondering how this would affect the direction of his writing.

We did not see Nathalie again. Martin returned to the cottage, pale and sorrowful, keeping indoors for the most part and then leaving suddenly in his car at two or three in the morning to, I suspected, walk through the fields until dawn. Many weeks later he knocked at my door and told me, over several whiskies, that Nathalie had not only lost their baby but been told by the doctors that she could never have another. In the aftermath of her depression and grief, she had decided to leave him.

'But I love her so much,' he said. 'How could this all have happened? Why did she try to kill herself? What had I done?'

'You mean she didn't tell you?'

'She did keep saying she had never been unfaithful to me. But it hadn't occurred to me for a minute that she had.'

Someone had to explain, and there was no one but me to do it. 'Martin.' I put my hand on his shoulder. 'People in the village were saying that you weren't the father of the baby.'

He stared at me and I saw on his face the look I had not seen since he first met Nathalie, the ruthless look of someone determined to get somewhere, whatever the cost.

'Guy?' he said.

I nodded.

'They've been friends for years,' he said tiredly. 'It was Nathalie who persuaded him to make the programme about me. I don't suppose the gossips round here can understand that a man and a woman can be friends without wanting to sleep together.'

'Perhaps not.'

'I don't suppose those old bitches give a damn about the fact that they've ruined two lives,' he said savagely. 'It *was* the Pettifer woman, wasn't it?'

'Uh . . .'

'And that old phoney, Maggie Underwood?'

'Phoney?'

'Of course she is. Stands out a mile off. Was she in on it?'

I gave a small nod, as though hoping that its size would somehow fail to underline the enormity of what had happened.

'I thought so,' Martin said. 'And no doubt Jean Wallace was in on it too. Nathalie told me she and Guy had bumped into her once in some restaurant.'

What I didn't understand was why Nathalie herself should have cared so much what the village thought about her. After all, she could have moved away. There was enough money for her and Martin to have lived anywhere. Perhaps it was the underlying neuroticism of her character that led her to make such an overly dramatic gesture. Or perhaps it was – I have often wondered since – guilt.

I thought Martin might move away but he stayed. He even began to take part in village affairs, something he had always surlily avoided before. I noticed that Tim Pettifer was a frequent caller and was glad: I myself was preoccupied both with writing my next book and handling the publicity attendant on the latest, since my publishers had finally decided to give me something of a push. It seemed to me, in the moments that I could spare to think about Martin, that he could do with a friend, even if it was someone so much younger. And as the only child of a possessive mother, Tim himself might benefit from a dose of the Fensome cynicism.

Soon, the village settled down again into its safely dull routines. Christmas would soon be on us, with all that meant of carol services, church decorations, parties and present-buying.

I wasn't aware for some time that anything was wrong. Then, in the first week in December, I realised that I had not received my invitation to the Wallace's party. Ordinarily I would simply have assumed that they had decided not to give it this year, even though the Wallace party was as eternal a fixture in the village year as the Parish picnic or the Conservative fête. But only a couple of months before, Jean herself had told me that they had decided to have a caterer this year.

I am naturally diffident. No invitation did not mean no party, merely that I myself had been excluded from it. Perhaps it was my determination not to feel hurt that made me more conscious of the

Wallaces than usual. I noticed that Ken's car was hardly ever at home these days. I noticed how often the house was unlit at night, as though no one was in. I even noticed that Jean was hardly ever seen.

It was Martin who enlightened me. 'What?' he said. 'You, of all people, haven't heard?'

'Heard what?'

'That Ken Wallace wants a divorce.'

It is difficult to explain the shock this news gave me. The Wallaces were so much part of the village that, in a sense, they almost *were* the village. If they were to part, then surely the village itself could no longer hold together but must inevitably be rent asunder. 'But they can't split up,' I said.

'Why on earth not?' He laughed his harsh laugh. 'They're no different from anyone else.'

There was no point in saying that in fact they were; that the two of them, solid, bougeois, comfortable, represented a kind of English goodness that was lacking in most people and must therefore be cherished at all costs. 'I can't believe it,' I said.

'You'd better. The house is up for sale, I understand.'

'You mean they're both leaving here?'

'They'll have to. The way I heard it, there are money problems. They'll both have to live at a considerably lower level apart than they managed together. Jean's been looking at flats in Larton, so I understand.'

'Larton? But that's a dreadful place.'

'I suppose it's all she can afford.'

'But why is Ken doing this? Is there another woman?'

'As far as I know, it's Jean. She's been having an affair with someone.'

I stared at him stupidly. '*Jean!*'

'That's what I was told. They were seen in London, apparently.'

'Who by?'

He shrugged. 'I can't remember. Perhaps it was the man she was having dinner with when she spotted Nathalie with Guy.'

Jean of course, denied it. I visited her in Larton, a horrid little industrial suburb. The flat was uncomfortable and cold; even the furniture and possessions she brought with her failed to make it anything but unpleasant. She spent most of my visit weeping, her broad frame jammed into the corner of a couch from their old house that was far too big for the poky little room. 'As if I would have an affair,' she sobbed. 'I love Kenneth, why would I want to? Besides,' and she looked away from me out of the window where factory chimneys dominated the grubby back gardens, 'I don't even like . . .' Her voice trailed away.

'Like what?'

'You know . . . sex.'

There was little I could say to this. The thought of Ken and Jean in bed together was unsettling enough: to envisage them coupling was a little more than I wanted to contemplate. 'Does Ken know?'

'Well . . .' She looked uncomfortable.

'Does he seriously believe you were having an affair?' I tried to keep my own incredulity out of my voice.

'Apparently he does. And he says, even if I wasn't, the damage has been done now, and a man in his position can't afford to have rumours going round about his wife. Better to divorce, he says, than be a laughing-stock.'

I could imagine him saying that. Ken did not have much sense of humour and would not relish innuendo about his wife. But I still could not understand where the rumour began in the first place.

'Somebody saw me,' Jean said, when I asked. 'In L'Escargot. And Ken refuses to believe that I was there alone, although I was.'

'Doing what?'

'Just eating. That's all. Just eating.'

She saw my bewilderment. 'It was after all those years of cooking for others,' she said hurriedly. 'Fish fingers and hot dogs for the children, and Ken wanting roasts with two veg. And now he's gone all health-conscious: wheat-germ and raw carrots all the time. I wanted to eat something delicious I hadn't cooked myself. I wanted to have it served to me, for a change. That's all.'

As I was leaving, she clutched my arm. 'It's all happened so quickly,' she said. Her face was swollen, fatter than it had been, unmade-up. She looked ugly. Worse than that, she looked frightened. 'One minute I was happy. Now . . .' She looked back along the mean passage to the mean little sitting room. 'I don't think I ever will be again.'

'Of course you will. You mustn't talk like that.'

'No.' She shook her head.

'You'll see.'

'No,' she said again. She opened the front door, a horrid affair of fluted glass and plywood. 'Thank you for coming. I haven't seen either Laura or Maggie since . . .'

The idea of Maggie Underwood sipping tea in that nasty little flat, her long leather gloves spread on her knee, was too ludicrous to contemplate. I would have expected Laura to be kinder.

But Laura had troubles of her own. As though the Wallace divorce was the beginning of a larger rupture, a further crack in the fabric of our peaceful lives, Tim Pettifer suddenly decided to throw up accountancy and head for India or Israel or somewhere.

He came and lounged restlessly in front of my fire, telling me about it. 'I mean, it's all so pointless,' he said, 'so meaningless. I mean, I slog away for three years and then do another three or four years further training, and there I am, a boring accountant or economist or banker or something for the rest of my life.'

'I thought that's what you wanted to be.'

'Yeah, well . . .' he said. He stood up and kicked at a log protruding from the fire. 'I did, once. But . . . I don't know. I'm older now: I don't want to shut all the doors before I've even been through them, do I?'

I'd heard Martin once express a similar opinion. 'Have you discussed this with Martin?' I said.

'Sort of.' He lifted his shoulders in the uncouth way that the young do. 'Like he says, what's life all about, when you get down to it? Sitting at a desk, earning a salary?' The sneer he gave this last word was magnificent.

'Do you have an alternative in mind?'

'Yeah, well, I want to see a bit of the world first, don't I? Live a bit, get away from my mother, apart from anything else.'

'That's rather cruel, Tim.'

'It's like Martin says, she's been smothering me all my life,' he burst out. 'I want to live my own way, not hers. And when I get back, I don't want to settle down into some kind of stultifying job, just so I can keep her in luxury in her old age.'

'What a terrible thing to say.'

'Yeah, well,' he said, ungraciously. 'I happen to think it's true.'

'But she's scraped and scrimped so you would be properly educated, have all the opportunities you could need.'

'I never asked for them,' he said, not meeting my eye. 'Anyway, I want to make my own opportunities. Or not. As the case may be.'

Poor Laura. With Tim gone, her ebullience seemed to vanish. Her hair did not turn white overnight but certainly six months later it was so much greyer than it had been and her figure so stooped that, seeing her in the distance crossing the village green, I took her for a moment to be an old woman, a stranger.

But it was the revelation about Maggie Underwood which concerned us all by then. It appeared that the General's memoirs did not exist, that Maggie's trips to London to visit the editor at his publishing house were in fact a figment of her imagination.

Worse was to follow: it turned out that the General himself was a fictional character in the slim volume that – so it transpired – was Maggie's life. Far from being the daughter of a high-ranking military officer, she had been born in some back street in Bolton, the illegitimate daughter of a midwife who had later married a supply clerk at the nearby Army depot. As Martin said, taking a glass of whisky with me one evening shortly after we heard, it was not so much the lie that was astonishing, as the fact that she bothered to tell it.

'Why should we care?' he said. 'There's nothing wrong with being illegitimate, let alone in having a midwife for a mother.' He laughed hurtfully. 'Though I too might have been tempted to keep quiet about Bolton!'

'Poor Maggie,' I said. 'This will destroy her.'

'Serve her right, if you ask me. All that snobby nonsense about taking tea with her, and the endless crap about the General. No wonder the village is laughing its head off.'

'Is it such a sin to embroider a little?' I asked.

'Yes,' he said. His jaw was hard. 'If it hurts other people.'

'Maggie's little fictions can't have hurt anyone at all.'

'Perhaps not the ones about her father,' he said viciously.

*

It was not more than three days later that Maggie Underwood drank the contents of a plastic bottle of bleach purchased from the village shop. I've spent hours since, especially on sleepless nights, trying not to imagine how painful a death it must have been for her, lying there on the kitchen floor while the soft tissues inside her disintegrated.

Shortly after that, a FOR SALE sign appeared on the cottage next door. A young couple expecting their first baby bought it; they seemed nice enough from what I could see, and excited about living in a house once owned by a Major British Novelist. For that, thanks partly to Guy Henderson's television programme, was what Martin had now become.

When the pantechnicon had carted away his furniture – he had bought a large flat in Kensington from the proceeds of the film rights of his most recent book – I went down my own garden path and up his. He was sitting on one of the window seats, waiting for the new owners to arrive so that he could hand over the key.

'I would have come to say goodbye,' he said.

'I know.'

'In spite of . . . everything. I'm sorry to be leaving.'

'Well,' I said, and I hoped my own sense of loss and destruction did not show too much, though the novelist's eye is an acute and penetrating one. 'It's no longer the village you came to, is it?'

The expression on his face sharpened as he looked at me. 'I suppose it's not.'

I wondered if he was really able to assess the damage done, or saw it merely as a kind of wild justice. 'It will be interesting to see whether it makes you a better writer,' I said.

'How do you mean?'

'Now that you can write out of personal experience of what it's like to commit a crime,' I said.

Before he could answer, I turned round and walked through his gate and back through mine and up the path to my front door. I stepped inside and closed it behind me.

K. K.

Liza Cody

Let me tell you something: on a hot day at Fantasyland life can be hell for King Kong. You have to wear long johns for the itching, and by the end of the day they're soaked. I lost pounds on sunny days. Not that it showed. A woman my size has to lose stones for it to make any real difference.

I'm not complaining. If you take all the facts into consideration I was lucky to have the job. The facts, of course, are my face and figure.

I was always going to be tall. When the accident happened I was thirteen years old and already five foot ten.

It's no handicap to be tall. There are plenty of models and basketball players over six feet. But after the accident I began to eat, for comfort really, and you can't comfort yourself to the extent I did without putting on a lot of weight.

King Kong, at the beginning, was supposed to be a man. But I got the job because I was the only one who fitted the costume. King Kong is a star. I hadn't even applied for King Kong. No, my hopes were pinned on Hettie Hamburger, one of the cafeteria troupe. But at the last moment, only a couple of days before the grand opening, they switched me with Louis.

Louis, they said, was a little too limp to make a convincing King Kong. 'All the rehearsal in the world won't turn that nancy into a plausible monster,' the artistic director said. They think just because they can't see our faces we can't hear what's said about us. But we can.

'What's that hulking great hamburger doing at the end of the line?' he said, when he came to inspect the cafeteria. 'You can't have a threatening hamburger. It'll put the kiddies off their food.'

I thought it was the end for me. If you fail as a hamburger there's not a lot of hope left. But the artistic director, thank heaven, had a little imagination. 'See if she can get into K. K.,' he said.

I could. 'Terrific,' the artistic director said. 'Dynamite. Put her by the gate for the opening. She's a natural.'

We opened very successfully with me and the Creature from the Black Lagoon welcoming the crowds. The kiddies screamed and giggled as I lolloped around growling. They wanted to stroke my fur and have their pictures taken with me.

I can't tell you how lovely this is for someone like me. Without a monster costume no one wants to take my picture at all, and the kiddies cross the road rather than come face to face with me on the pavement. I love kiddies, but I've got to be realistic. It's unlikely I'll ever have any of my own. Children are frightened by disfigurement and it's one of life's little ironies that they have only come to love me now that it's my job to frighten them. I'm a wonderful monster if I do say it myself. Who would have thought that someone like me could succeed in show business?

But it isn't like that for everyone. My friend, Cherry, for instance, used to get very depressed. 'I'm a dancer,' she used to tell me. 'A good dancer. Well, quite a good dancer. Not a bloody hot dog. It's an insult, even if I am over thirty.'

She's over forty, actually, but she's right: she's still very pretty in spite of being a little on the plump side. It's a shame to hide her in a hot dog.

'I'll give that agent of mine a piece of my mind,' she used to say, 'you see if I don't.' Well, maybe she did or maybe she didn't. The only thing I know is that two years later she's still a hot dog, and a good one at that. She says the tips are getting better all the time. She doesn't positively enjoy the job the way I did, but she doesn't complain much any more.

Performers at Fantasyland divide up quite neatly into Freaks and Food, and I think it's fair to say that of the two the Freaks are happier in their work. They are the entertainers and the extroverts.

But they are quite territorially minded too. I had a jungle, about half an acre of mixed conifers and rhododendron bushes with a climbing frame artfully disguised as creeping vines. You wouldn't catch Godzilla in my domain. He roams the area around the gift shop while the boating pool belongs to the Beast from 20,000 Fathoms.

Of course, some of the Freaks work in teams. The Tingle-Trail is a miniature railway ride which begins in the Black Forest with the Werewolves in their various stages of transformation and ends in a graveyard with a stunning display by the Zombies, the Undead and a pair of Bodysnatchers. There are twenty-three employed on the Tingle-Trail alone, and they have to work to a strict timetable.

The others give improvised performances. We all perfected the art of lurking and popping up unexpectedly. It is a delicate balance: shrieks of shock and surprise are the signs of a job well done but you don't want to scare anyone into a heart attack. There have been accidents, and we learned to watch out, especially for grandparents. The kiddies are pretty resilient; they want to be terrified. But the grandparents can be rather more fragile.

Although we rarely witnessed each other's performances, there was a lot of respect around for the way each of us coped with our working conditions. I'd say, for instance, that the Mummy had the most difficult job. The Egyptian Tomb is a maze and a maze is claustrophobic. The Mummy was one of those men who could make something out of nothing. He stayed very still, and when he moved it was almost imperceptible. It was as if he was playing Grandmother's Footsteps with his audience. He terrified his visitors slowly and subtly and I must say that of all of us he was the one I admired most.

Mummy used to sing with the Scottish Opera until asthma ruined his career. He was an enormous man, but unlike me he did not work out with weights. He didn't have to: physical strength was not part of his act. Timing was his forte. I wish I had seen him on stage – with that size and presence coupled with his sense of timing he must have been quite electric. Mummy was an artist and an outstandingly gentle person so we all felt his humiliation personally.

It happened late one June evening. The ticket office had been closed for an hour and the last visitors were trickling away. I had come down from my climbing frame and was beginning to make my way over to the dressing room when a pack of teenage boys burst out of the Egyptian Tomb and chased each other to the exit. I noticed with alarm that one of them was waving a piece of burning cloth.

Fire is something we were all trained to look out for, and my first thought was that a member of the public might be trapped in the maze. I rushed in calling for the attendant to turn on the house lights. I did not know the tomb very well and I could not waste time running around in the dark searching for a fire extinguisher.

I found Mummy on his back, his costume slashed and his feet smouldering. Smoke and shock had caused an asthma attack. He was in a bad way.

I put the fire out immediately. But it was difficult to get his headpiece off. I had to free my own hands first. My King Kong costume is not designed for dainty work and I wear huge furry gauntlets. We were in a confined space and Mummy is a big man but I managed at last. His lips were turning mauve.

An asthmatic finds it difficult to breathe lying down. I should have propped him up straight away. But his costume was stiff and bulky. Luckily an attendant arrived and together we managed to pull apart the intricate system of Velcro and zips which held it together.

Mummy was not badly hurt. His feet were scorched and that was about all. But I could not help thinking about what it must have been like for him trapped in his own tomb, imprisoned in his winding sheet.

The costume had been the provocation. Apparently the boys had wanted to unwrap Mummy. They had become angry and violent when they found they couldn't.

As I say, what we all felt most keenly was the humiliation. Nosferatu put it best. 'It's the role reversal,' he said. 'They aren't supposed to frighten us. We're supposed to frighten them.'

That made me think. 'But it's all an illusion,' I said.

'That's right, K. K.,' said Nosferatu. 'It's all in their minds that we can frighten them so they give us the power to frighten them. Once they stop playing their parts we can't play ours, and shebang! – it's all over.'

It was a conversation I kept remembering in the days that followed. A local newspaper got hold of Mummy's story and from that time on our public seemed to change.

For one thing there weren't so many little kiddies. I suppose the parents and grandparents were afraid of exposing them to hooligans. And there were definitely more hooligans. Incident followed incident. Charley, The Fly, had his wings torn off. Godzilla's tail was hacked to pieces with carpet knives. A gang of youths tried to electrocute the Bride of Frankenstein. We were being persecuted.

How strange, I thought. Because when you go back to most of the original stories we monsters only became monstrous to defend ourselves against human persecution. King Kong is a good example. Kong was only trying to defend the tiny creature he loved and that's why a lot of people leave the movie feeling sorry for him. This is because *King Kong* is not a horror film. It is a romance. Not many people understand that. But they feel it. And it was always an important aspect of my characterisation to combine King Kong's raw power with tenderness. It wasn't difficult: I think I've mentioned already that I love little kiddies.

No one could call Cherry the motherly type, but even she missed the children. 'I don't know, K,' she said. 'If I've got to be laughed at I'd rather it was the little ones than these spotty erks. They just don't know how to have a good time without hurting someone.'

How right she was. Again, it happened in the evening. They came, five of them, just as my last visitors were leaving. They had hair so short you could see the tattoos on their skulls, and their trousers were tucked into army boots.

They ran in, beating down the rhododendrons with their sticks, yelling, 'Where's the sodding monkey?'

I stayed where I was on the climbing frame. I hoped my little family would escape quietly and go for help. But they stood there transfixed. There were three small children, I remember, all under seven. Their mother was with them, and the old man was probably her father. Very sweet, they had been, taking pictures of me holding the smallest child with the two older ones on either side. I didn't want them to come to any harm.

Fortunately the hooligans hardly noticed them. They clubbed the base of the climbing frame with their sticks. They tried to shake me off.

'Hoo-hoo-hoo!' they screamed. 'Come down and we'll give you

some nuts.' I didn't move. They could shake that frame all night and it wouldn't budge.

'We'll give it some nuts all right,' they said. 'If it won't get down and fight like a monkey we'll drag it down.'

They swarmed up my frame. They swung on my ropes. I went from level to level to avoid them. If only the family had gone for help – if only the hooligans had been stupid – I might have got away with it.

But it only takes one with a bit of intelligence to organise the other four into a dangerous unit. He was small. He was neat. He had clear blue eyes which blazed with excitement. He was one of those lads who love a challenge. My agility on the climbing frame was a challenge. It became a competition he wanted to win.

He set three of them to drive me to the edge of the frame. The other he put on a rope. As I prepared to haul myself up to the next level he sprung his trap.

'Now!' he screamed.

The lad on the rope swung. I saw him coming but there was nowhere to go. He hit me like an iron pendulum and I flew off the frame and went crashing to the ground. The others dropped on me. I thought my back was broken.

They sorted themselves out soon enough. 'Let's see the bastard,' the leader said. 'Get his fucking mask off.'

They tore King Kong's face off mine and threw it into the bushes.

'Shit!' they said. 'Bloody hell! Look at that.'

The little children, who up till then had only been crying, started to scream.

I can hardly bear to remember what happened next. I suppose it reminds me too painfully of the past. You see, after the accident, after my face healed, my mother decided that it would be best for me to have plastic surgery to put things right. So I went back into hospital where they broke my cheekbones again and tried to rearrange my eye socket. But something went wrong. It does sometimes. It wasn't anyone's fault. Maybe I rejected my own tissue.

My mother had begun hopefully but after the failure it became harder and harder for the doctors to comfort her. In the end, she took my little sister and went north to Scotland and I never saw her again. It was a relief in a way. Because as she became unable to stand the sight of my face, I became unable to stand the sight of hers. Well, not her face, exactly, more the expression on it. I don't have to look at myself, but I do have to look at the people who are looking at me. I know I am a fright, and when people look at me they become ugly too.

The last line in the movie *King Kong* is: "Twas beauty killed the beast.' Well, in my experience, it's the other way round. When even the prettiest people look at me they become horrible, so the beast kills beauty.

The little kiddies screamed.

The lad with the clear blue eyes said, 'Shit! No wonder it wears a monkey suit.'

'Come on,' he said, 'Let's get out of here before I throw up.'

I got up. I couldn't find my mask. I took off my gauntlets. I hit him on the side of his handsome head, and when he was down I dropped on his throat with all my weight.

You know, sometimes you find a piece of backbone in a tin of salmon, and when you get it between your teeth it breaks with a soft crunching sound. It was as easy as that.

I shouldn't have done it. I was bigger than him. He was only a kid really – not a child any more but not grown-up either. But at the time it seemed to me he had taken away everything that was mine. All I had was an illusion anyway – the illusion of being a monster. You can't kill someone for that. It just isn't enough.

The funny thing is how nice everyone was about it – even the police. 'I understand,' everyone kept saying. They look at my face and they say, 'I understand,' as if my face tells them everything, as if a disfigured face clearly explains an ugly action. Even the doctors, who are educated men and should know better, think it was years of taunts and rejection which drove me to murder. My solicitor tells me he's sure the court will accept a plea of self-defence. 'They'll understand,' he says confidently.

What if I tell the court I just lost my temper? Suppose I tell them, as I'm telling you, that my face doesn't represent me any more than yours does you? My face is an accident, but I am responsible for my actions. A sad life and an ugly face do not make me any less responsible for losing my temper, do they?

Perhaps they really think I'm King Kong, that I'm not quite

human. Just as they feel sorry for King Kong, because although he's a monster he seems to feel human emotions, so they feel sorry for me. If they really thought I was human they'd deal with me the same way they dealt with that man who murdered his girlfriend last month because she threw a plate of baked beans in his face. They don't tell him they understand.

But look on the bright side. Fantasyland has a new regulation now and teenagers are not allowed in unless accompanied by a little child. Apart from that Cherry says it's business as usual. She says it's not the same without me though, and she doesn't think the man who took over my job will last the summer.

'He complains like anything on sunny days,' she told me last time she visited. 'He's got eczema and the itching drives him crazy.'

Cherry should know. Life can be hell for a hot dog too on a sunny day. You don't have to be King Kong to suffer.

LETTER TO HIS SON

Simon Brett

Parkhurst
16th June, 1986

DEAR BOY,

I am sorry to hear the Fourth of June celebrations was a trial. I've used that agency before and they never give me no trouble, but I will certainly withdraw my future custom after this lot, and may indeed have to send the boys round. Honest, Son, I asked them to send along a couple what would really raise you in your fellow-Etonians' esteem when they saw who you got for parents. I had to get Blue Phil to draw quite a lot out of the old deposit account under the M23/M25 intersection, and I just don't reckon I got value for my hard-earned oncers.

OK, the motor was all right. Vintage Lagonda must've raised a few eyebrows. Pity it was hot. Still, you can't have everything. But really . . . To send along Watchstrap Malone and Berwick Street Barbara as your mum and dad is the height of naffness so far as yours truly is concerned. I mean, doesn't no one have any finesse these days? No, it's not good enough. I'm afraid there's going to be a few broken fingers round that agency unless I get a strongly worded apology in folded form.

For a start, why did they send a villain to be *in loco parentis*? (See, I am not wasting my time down the prison library.) Are they under new management? Always when I used them in the past, they sent along actors, people with no form. Using Watchstrap, whose record's as long as one of Barry Manilow's *sounds*, is taking unnecessary risks. OK, he looks the toff, got the plummy voice and

all that, but he ISN'T THE GENUINE ARTICLE. Put him in a marquee with an authentic Eton dad and the other geezer's going to
see he's not the business within thirty seconds. Remember, in
matters of class, THERE'S NO WAY SOMEONE WHO ISN'T CAN
EVER PASS HIMSELF OFF AS THE REAL THING (a point which I
will return to later in this letter).

And, anyway, if they was going to send a villain, least they could
have done was to send a good one. Watchstrap Malone, I'll have you
know, got his cognomen (prison library again) from a case anyone
would wish to draw a veil over, when he was in charge of hijacking a
container-load of what was supposed to be watches from Heathrow.
Trouble was, he only misread the invoice, didn't he? Wasn't the
watches, just the blooming straps. Huh, not the kind of form suitable
to someone who's going to pass themselves off as any son of mine's
father.

And as for using Berwick Street Barbara, well, that's just a straight
insult to your mother, isn't it? I mean, I know she's got the posh voice
and the clothes, but she's not the real thing any more than Watchstrap is. She gets her business from nasty little common erks who think
they're stepping up a few classes (been quite a boom in that line of
business since this Princess of Wales been all over the newspapers).
But no genuine Horray Henry'd be fooled by Barbara. Anyway, that
lot don't want all the quacking vowels and the headscarves – get
enough of that at home. What they're after in that line is some pert
little scrubber dragged out of the gutters of Toxteth. But I digress.

Anyway, like I say, it's an insult to your mother and if she ever gets
to hear about it, I wouldn't put money on the roof staying on
Holloway.

No, I'm sorry, I feel like I've been done, and last time I felt like
that, with Micky 'The Cardinal' O'Riordhan, he ended up having a
lot more difficulty in kneeling down than what he had had thereto-
fore.

But now, Son, I come on to the more serious part of this letter. I was
not amused to hear what your division master said about your work. If
you've got the idea in your thick skull that being a toff has anything to
do with sitting on your backside and doing buggerall, then it's an idea
of which you'd better disabuse yourself sharpish.

I haven't put in all the time (inside and out) what I have to pay for your education with a view to you throwing it all away. It's all right for an authentic scion (prison library) of the aristocracy to drop out of the system; the system will cheerfully wait till he's ready to go back in. But someone in your shoes, Sonny, if you drop out, you stay out.

Let me clarify my position. Like all fathers, I want my kids to have things better than I did. Now, I done all right. I'm not complaining. I've got to the top of my particular tree. There's still a good few pubs round the East End what'll go quiet when my name's mentioned and, in purely material terms, with the houses in Tenerife and Jamaica and Friern Barnet (not to mention the stashes under various bits of the country's motorway network), I am, to put it modestly, comfortable.

But – and this is a big but – in spite of my career success, I remain an old-fashioned villain. My methods – and I'm not knocking them, because they work – are, in the ultimate analysis, crude. All right, most people give you what you want if you hit them hard enough, but that system of business has not changed since the beginning of time. Nowadays, there is no question, considerably more sophisticated methods are available to the aspiring professional.

Computers obviously have made a big difference. The advance of microtechnology has made possible that elusive goal, the perfect crime, in which you just help yourself without getting your hands dirty.

For this reason I was *particularly* distressed to hear that you haven't been paying attention in your computer studies classes. Listen, Son, I am paying a great deal to put you through Eton and (I think we can safely assume after the endowment for the new library block) Cambridge, but if at the end of all that you emerge unable to fiddle a computerised bank account, I am going to be less than chuffed. Got it?

However, what I'm doing for you is not just with a view to you getting *au fait* with the new technology. It's more than that.

OK, like I say, I been successful, and yet the fact remains that here I am writing to you from the nick. Because my kind of operation, being a straightforward villain against the system, will never be without its attendant risks. Of which risks the nick is the biggest one.

You know, being in prison does give you time for contemplation, and, while I been here, I done a lot of thinking about the inequalities of the society in which we live.

I mean, say I organise a security van hijack, using a dozen heavies, with all the risks involved (bruises from the pickaxe handles, whiplash injuries from ramming the vehicle, being shopped by one of my own team, being traced through the serial numbers, to name but a few), what do I get at the end of it? I mean, after it's all been shared out, after I've paid everyone off, bribed a few, sorted out pensions for the ones who got hurt, all that, what do I get?' Couple of hundred grand if I'm lucky.

Whereas some smartarse in the City can siphon off that many million in a morning without stirring from his desk (and in many cases without even technically breaking the law).

Then, if I'm caught, even with the most expensive solicitor in London acting for me, I get twelve years in Parkhurst.

And, if he's caught, what does he get? Maybe has to resign from the board. Maybe has to get out the business and retire to his country estate, where he lives on investment income and devotes himself to rural pursuits, shooting, fishing, being a JP, that sort of number.

Now, I ask myself, is that a fair system?

And the answer, of course, doesn't take long to come back. No.

Of course it isn't fair. It never has been. That's why I've always voted Tory. All that socialist rubbish about trying to 'change society' . . . huh. It's never going to change. The system is as it is. Which is why, to succeed you got to go *with* the system, rather than *against* it.

Which brings me, of course, to what I'm doing for you.

By the time you get through Eton and Cambridge, Son, the world will be your oyster. Your earning potential will be virtually unlimited.

Now don't get me wrong. I am not suggesting that you should go straight. Heaven forbid. No son of mine's going to throw away five generations of tradition just like that.

No, what I'm suggesting is, yes, you're still a villain, but you're a villain from *inside* the system. I mean, think of the opportunities you'll have. You'll be able to go into the City, the Law . . . we could use a bent solicitor in the family . . . even, if you got *really* lucky, into Parliament. And let's face it, in any of those professions, you're going to clean up in a way that'll make my pickaxe-and-bovver approach look as old-fashioned as a slide-rule in the days of calculators.

Which is why it is so, so important that you take your education seriously. You have got to come out the genuine article. Never relax. You're not there just to do the academic business, you got to observe your classmates too. Follow their every move. Do as they do. You can get to the top, Son (not just in the country, in the world – all big businesses are going multinational these days), but for you to get there you got to be the real thing. No chinks in your armour – got that? Many highly promising villains have come unstuck by inattention to detail and I'm determined it shouldn't happen to you.

Perhaps I can best clarify what I'm on about by telling you what happened to old Squiffy Yoxborough.

Squiffy was basically a con-merchant. Used to be an actor, specialised in upper-class parts. Hadn't got any real breeding, brought up in Hackney as a matter of fact, but he could do the voice real well and, you know, he'd studied the type. Made a kind of speciality of an upper-class drunk act, pretending to be pissed, you know. Hence the name, Squiffy. But times got hard, the acting parts wasn't there, so he drifted into our business.

First of all, he never did anything big. Main speciality was borrowing the odd fifty at upper-class piss-ups. Henley, Ascot, hunt balls, that kind of number, he'd turn up in the full fig and come the hard-luck story when the guests had been hitting the champers for a while. He sounded even more smashed than them, but of course he knew exactly where all his marbles was.

It was slow money, but fairly regular, and moving with that crowd opened up other possibilities. Nicking the odd bit of jewellery, occasional blackmail, a bit of 'winkling' old ladies out of their flats for property developers, you know what I mean. Basically, just doing the upper-classes' dirty work. There's always been a demand for people to do that, and I dare say there always will be.

Well, inevitably, this led pretty quick to drugs. When London's full of Hooray Henries wanting to stick stuff up their ancestral noses, there's bound to be a lot of openings for the pushers, and Squiffy took his chances when they come. He was never in the big league, mind, not controlling the business, just a courier and like point-of-sale merchant. But it was better money, and easier, than sponging fifties.

Incidentally, Son, since the subject's come up, I don't want there to be any doubt in your mind about my views on drugs. You keep away from them.

Now, I am not a violent man – well, let's say I am not a violent man to my *family*, but if I hear you've been meddling with drugs, either as a user or a pusher, so help me I will somehow get out of this place and find you and give you such a tanning with my belt that you'll need a rubber ring for the rest of your natural. That sort of business attracts a really unpleasant class of criminal what I don't want any son of mine mixing with. Got that?

Anyway, getting back to Squiffy, obviously once he got into drugs, he was going to get deeper in and pretty soon he's involved with some villains who was organising the smuggling of the stuff through a yacht charter company. You know the sort of set-up, rich gits rent this boat and crew and swan round the West Indies for a couple of weeks, getting alternately smashed and stoned.

Needless to say, this company would keep their punters on the boat supplied with cocaine; but not only that, they also made a nice little business of taking the stuff back into England and flogging it to all the Sloane Rangers down the Chelsea discothèques.

I suppose it could have been a good little earner if you like that kind of thing, but these plonkers who was doing it hadn't got no sense of organisation. The crew were usually as stoned as the punters, so it was only a matter of time before they come unstuck. Only third run they do, they moor in the harbour of this little island in the West Indies and, while they're all on shore getting well bobbled on the ethnic rum, local Bill goes and raids the yacht. Stuff's lying all over the place, like there's been a snow-storm blown through the cabins, and when the crew and punters come back, they all get nicked and shoved in the local slammer to unwind for a bit.

Not a nice place, the gaol on this little island. They had to share their cells with a nasty lot of local fauna like cockroaches, snakes and mosquitoes, not to mention assorted incendiaries, gun-runners, rapists and axe-murderers.

Not at all what these merchant bankers and their Benenden-educated crumpet who had chartered the yacht was used to. So, because that's how things work at that level, pretty soon some British consular official gets contacted, and pretty soon a deal gets struck with the local authorities. No hassle, really, it comes down to a thousand quid per prisoner. All charges dropped, and home they go. Happened all the time, apparently. The prisons was one of the island's two most lucrative industries (the other being printed unperforated stamps). A yacht had only to come into the harbour to get raided. Squiffy's lot had just made it easy for the local police; usually the cocaine had to be planted.

Well, obviously, there was a lot of transatlantic telephoning, a lot of distraught daddies (barristers, MPs, what-have-you) cabling money across, but it gets sorted out pretty quick and all the Hoorays are flown back to England with a good story to tell at the next cocktail party.

They're all flown back, that is, except Squiffy.

And it wasn't that he couldn't raise the readies. He'd got a few stashes round about, and the odd blackmail victim who could be relied on to stump up a grand when needed.

No, he stayed because he'd met this bloke in the nick.

Don't get me wrong. I don't mean he fancied him. Nothing Leaning Tower of Pisa about Squiffy.

No, he stayed, because he'd met someone he thought could lead to big money.

Bloke's name was Masters. Alex Masters. But, it didn't take Squiffy long to find out, geezer was also known as the Marquess of Gorsley.

Now, I don't know how it is, but some people always land on their feet in the nick. I mean, I do all right. I get all the snout I want and if I feel like a steak or a bottle of whisky there's no problem. But I get that because I have a bit of reputation outside, and I have to work to keep those privileges. I mean, if there wasn't a good half dozen heavies round the place who owe me the odd favour, I might find it more difficult.

But I tell you, I got nothing compared to what this marquess geezer'd got. Unlimited supplies of rum, so he's permanently smashed, quietly and happily drinking himself to death. All the food he wants, very best of the local cuisine. Nice cell to himself, air-conditioning, fridge, video, compact disc player, interior-sprung bed. Pick of the local talent to share that bed with, all these slim, brown-legged beauties, different one every night, so Squiffy said (though apparently the old marquess was usually too pissed to do much about it).

Now, prisons work the same all over the world, so you take my word that I know what I'm talking about. Only one thing gets those kinds of privileges.

Money.

But pretty soon even Squiffy realises there's something not quite kosher with the set-up. I mean, this Gorsley bloke's not inside for anything particularly criminal. Just some fraud on a holiday villa development scheme. Even if the island's authorities take property fiddling more seriously than cocaine, there's still got to be a price to get him released. I mean, say it's five grand, it's still going to be considerably less than what he's paying per annum for these special privileges.

Besides, when Squiffy raises the subject, it's clear that the old marquess doesn't know a blind thing about this 'buy-out' system. But he does go on about how grateful he is to his old man, the Duke of Glammerton, for shelling out so much per month 'to make the life sentence bearable.'

Now Squiffy's not the greatest intellect since Einstein, but even he's capable of putting two and two together. He checks out this Gorsley geezer's form and discovers the property fraud's not the first bit of bovver he's been in. In fact, the bloke is a walking disaster area, his past littered with bounced cheques, petty theft, convictions for drunkenness, you name it. (I don't, incidentally, mean *real* crimes, the ones that involve skill; I refer to the sort people get into by incompetence.)

Squiffy does a bit more research. He's still got some cocaine stashed away and for that the prison governor's more than ready to spill the odd bean. Turns out the marquess's dad pays up regular, never objects when the price goes up, encourages the governor to keep increasing the supply of rum, states quite categorically he's not interested in pardons, anything like that. Seems he's got a nephew who's a real Mr Goody-Goody. And if the marquis dies in an alcoholic stupor in some obscure foreign jail, it's all very handy. The prissy nephew inherits the title, and the Family Name remains untarnished. Duke's prepared to pay a lot to keep that untarnished.

So it's soon clear to Squiffy that the duke is not only paying a monthly sum to keep his son in the style to which he's accustomed;

it's also to keep his son out of the country. In fact, he's paying the island to let the Marquess of Gorsley die quietly in prison.

It's when he realises this that Squiffy Yoxborough decides he'll stick around for a while.

Now, except for the aforementioned incendiaries, gun-runners, rapists and axe-murderers . . . oh, and the local talent (not that that talked much), the marquess has been a bit starved of civilised conversation, so he's pretty chuffed to be joined by someone who's English and talks with the right sort of accent. He doesn't notice that Squiffy's not the genuine article. Too smashed most of the time to notice anything and, since the marquess's idea of a conversation is him rambling on and someone else listening, Squiffy doesn't get too much chance to give himself away.

Anyway, he's quite content to listen, thank you very much. The more he finds out about the Marquess of Gorsley's background, the happier he is. It all ties in with a sort of plan that's slowly emerging in his head.

Particularly he wants to know about the marquess's schooldays. So, lots of warm, tropical evenings get whiled away over bottles of rum while the marquess drunkenly reminisces and Squiffy listens hard. It's really just an extension of how he started in the business, pretending to get plastered with the Hoorays. But this time he's after considerably more than the odd fifty.

The Marquess of Gorsley was, needless to say, at one of these really posh schools. Like his father before him, he had gone to Raspington in Wiltshire (near where your grandfather was arrested for the first time, Son). And as he listens, Squiffy learns all about it.

He learns that there was four houses, Thurrocks, Wilmington, Stuke and Fothergill. He learns that the marquess was in Stuke, that kids just starting in Stuke was called 'tads' and on their first night in the dorm they underwent 'scrogging'. He learns that prefects was called 'whisks', that in their common room, called 'the Treacle Tin', they was allowed to administer a punishment called 'spluggers'; that they could wear the top buttons of their jackets undone, and was the only members of the school allowed to walk on 'Straggler's Hump'.

He learns that the teachers was called 'dommies', that the sweet shop was called the 'Binn', that a cricket cap was a 'skiplid', that the bogs was called 'fruitbowls', that studies was called 'nitboxes', that lunch was called 'slops', and that a minor sports colours tie was called a 'slagnoose'.

He hears the marquess sing the school songs. After a time, he starts joining in with them. Eventually, he even gets a bit good at doing a solo on the School Cricket Song, traditionally sung in Big Hall on the evening after the Old Raspurian Match. It begins,

> Hark! the shout of a schoolboy at twilight
> Comes across from the far distant pitch,
> Goads his team on to one final effort,
> 'Make a stand at the ultimate ditch!'
> Hark! the voice of the umpiring master
> Rises over the white-flannelled strife,
> Tells his charges that life is like cricket,
> Tells them also that cricket's like life . . .

Don't think you have that one at Eton, do you, Son?

I tell you, after two months in that prison, Squiffy Yoxborough knows as much about being at Raspington as the Marquess of Gorsley does himself. He stays on a couple more weeks, to check there's nothing more, but by now the marquess is just rambling and repeating himself, sinking deeper and deeper into an alcoholic coma. So Squiffy quickly organises his own thousand quid release money, and scarpers back to England.

First thing he does when he gets back home, Squiffy forms a company. Well, he doesn't actually literally form a company, but he, like, gets all the papers forged so it looks like he's formed a company. He calls this company 'Only Real Granite House-Building Construction Techniques' (ORGHBCT) and he gets enough forged paperwork for him to be able to open a bank account in that name.

Next thing he gets his clothes together. Moves carefully here. Got to get the right gear or the whole thing falls apart.

Dark blue pinstripe suit. Donegal tweed suit. Beale and Inman corduroy trousers. Cavalry twills. Turnbull & Asser striped shirts. Viyella Tattersall checked shirts. Church's Oxford shoes. Barbour jacket. Herbert Johnson trilby.

He steals or borrows this lot. Can't just buy them in the shops. Got to look old, you see.

Has trouble with the Old Raspurian tie. Doesn't know anyone who went there – except of course for the marquess, and he's rather a long way away.

So he has to buy a tie new and distress it a bit. Washes it so's it shrinks. Rubs in a bit of grease. Looks all right.

(You may be wondering, Son, how I come to know all this detail. Not my usual special subject, I agree. Don't worry, all will be revealed.)

Right, so having got the gear, he packs it all in a battered old leather suitcase, rents a Volvo estate and drives up to Scotland.

He's checked out where the Duke of Glammerton's estate is, he's checked that the old boy's actually in residence, and he just drives up to the front of Glammerton House. Leaves the Volvo on the gravel, goes up to the main door and pulls this great ring for the bell.

Door's opened by some flunkey.

'Hello,' says Squiffy, doing the right voice of course. 'I'm a chum of Alex's. Just happened to be in the area. Wondered if the old devil was about.'

'Alex?' says the flunkey, bit suspicious.

'Yes. The Marquess of Gorsley. I was at school with him.'

'Ah. I'm afraid the marquess is abroad.'

'Oh really? What a swiz,' says Squiffy. 'Still, I travel a lot. Whereabouts is the old devil?'

Flunkey hesitates a bit, then says he'll go off and try to find out. Comes back with the butler. Butler confirms the marquess is abroad. Cannot be certain where.

'What, hasn't left a forwarding address? Always was bloody inefficient. Never mind, I'm sure some of my chums could give me a lead. Don't worry, I'll track him down.'

This makes the butler hesitate, too. 'If you'll excuse me, sir, I'll just go and see if his Grace is available. He might have more information about the marquess's whereabouts than I have.'

Few minutes later, Squiffy gets called into this big lounge-type room, you know, all deers' heads and gilt frames, and there's the

Duke of Glammerton sitting over a tray of tea. Duke sees the tie straight away.

'Good Lord, are you an Old Raspurian?'

'Yes, your Grace,' says Squiffy.

'Which house?'

'Stuke.'

'So was I.'

'Well, of course, Duke, I knew you must have been. That's where I met Alex, you see. Members of the same family in the same house, what?'

Duke doesn't look so happy now he knows Squiffy's a friend of his son. No doubt the old boy's met a few unsuitable ones in his time, so Squiffy says quickly, 'Haven't seen Alex for yonks. Virtually since school.'

'Oh.' Duke looks relieved. 'As Moulton said, I'm afraid he's abroad.'

'Living there?'

'Yes. For the time being,' Duke says carefully.

'Oh dear. You don't by any chance have an address, do you?'

'Erm . . . Not at the moment, no.'

Now all this is suiting Squiffy very nicely. The more the duke's determined to keep quiet about his son's real circumstances, the better.

'That's a nuisance,' says Squiffy. 'Wanted to sting the old devil for a bit of money.'

'Oh?' Duke looks careful again.

'Well, not for me, of course. For the old school.'

'Oh yes?' Duke looks interested.

'Absolutely.' (Squiffy knows he should say this every now and then instead of 'Yes'.) 'For my sins I've got involved in some fund-raising for the old place.'

'Again? What are they up to this time?'

'Building a new Great Hall to replace Big Hall.'

Duke's shocked by this. 'They're not going to knock Big Hall down?'

'Good Lord, no. No, Big Hall'll still be used. The Great Hall will be for school plays, that sort of thing.'

'Ah. Where are they going to build it?'

'Well, it'll be at right angles to Big Hall, sort of stretching past Thurrocks out towards Straggler's Hump.'

'Really? Good Lord.' The old geezer grins. 'I remember walking along "Straggler's Hump", many a time.'

'You must've been a "whisk" then.'

He looks guilty. 'Never was, actually.'

'Doing it illegally, were you?'

Duke nods.

'But didn't that mean you got dragged into the "Treacle Tin" for "spluggers"?'

'Never caught.' Duke giggles naughtily. 'Remember, actually, I did it my second day as a "tad".'

'What, directly after you'd been "scrogged"?'

'Absolutely.'

'And none of the "dommies" saw you?'

Duke shakes his head, really chuffed at what an old devil he used to be. 'Tell me,' he says, 'where are you staying up here?'

'I was going to check into the . . . what is it in the village? The Glammerton Arms?'

'Well, don't do that, old boy. Stay here the night. I'll get Moulton to show you a room.'

Gets a good dinner, that night, Squiffy does. Pheasant, venison, vintage wines, all that. Just the two of them. Duchess had died a long time ago.

Get on really well, they do. Squiffy does his usual getting-plastered act, but, as usual, he's careful. Talks a lot about Raspington, doesn't talk too much about the marquess. But listens. And gets confirmation of his hunch that the duke never wants to see his son again. Also knows there's a very strong chance of this happening in the natural course of events. The amount of rum the marquess is putting away, his liver must be shrivelled down to like a dried pea.

Anyway, when they're giving the port and brandy and cigars a bash, the duke, who's a bit worse for wear, says, 'What is all this about the old school? Trying to raise money, did you say?'

'Absolutely,' says Squiffy. 'Don't just want to raise money, though. Want to raise a monument.'

'What – a monument to all the chaps who died from eating "slops"?'

'Or the chaps who were poisoned in the "Binn"?'

'Or everyone who got "scrogged" in their own "nitbox"!'

'Yes, or all those who had a "down-the-loo-shampoo" in the "fruitbowls"!'

Duke finds this dead funny. Hasn't had such a good time for years.

'No, actually,' says Squiffy, all serious now, 'we want the new Great Hall to be a monument to a great Old Raspurian.'

'Ah.'

'So that every chap who walks into that hall will think of someone who was really a credit to the old school.'

'Oh. Got anyone in mind?' asks the Duke.

'Absolutely,' says Squiffy. 'We thought of Alex.'

'WHAT!'

'Well, he's such a great chap.'

'Alex – great chap?'

'Yes. As I say, I've hardly seen him since school . . . nor have any of the other fellows on the fund-raising committee, actually, but we all thought he was such a terrific chap at school . . . I mean, I'm sure he's gone on to be just as successful in the outside world.'

'Well . . . er . . .'

'So you see, Duke, we all thought, what a great idea to have the place named after Alex – I mean he'd have to put up most of the money, but that's a detail – and then everyone who went into the hall would be reminded of what a great Old Raspurian he was. Give the "tads" something to aspire to, what?'

'Yes, yes.' The Duke gets thoughtful. 'But are you sure that Alex is the right one?'

'Oh. Well, if there's any doubt about his suitability, perhaps we should investigate a bit further into what he's been up to since he left Raspington . . .'

'No, that won't be necessary,' says the duke, sharpish. 'What sort of sum of money are we talking about?'

'Oh . . .' Squiffy looks all casual, like. 'I don't know. Five hundred thousand, something like that.'

'Five hundred thousand to ensure that Alex is always remembered as one of the greatest Old Raspurians . . .?'

'I suppose you could think of it like that. Absolutely.'

A light comes into the old duke's eyes. He's had reports from the West Indies. He knows his son hasn't got long to go. And suddenly he's offered a way of . . . like *enshrining* the marquess's memory. With a great permanent monument at the old school, a little bit of adverse publicity in the past'll soon be forgotten. The Family Name will remain untarnished. Half a million's not much to pay for that.

He rings a bell and helps them both to some more pre-war port. Moulton comes in.

'My cheque book, please.'

The butler geezer delivers it and goes off again.

'Who should I make this payable to?' asks the duke.

'Well, in fact,' says Squiffy, 'the full name's the "Old Raspurian Great Hall Building Charitable Trust", but you'll never get all that on the cheque. Just the initials will do.'

With the cheque safely in his pocket, Squiffy starts humming the tune of the Raspington School Cricket Song.

'Great,' says the Duke. 'Terrific. I always used to do the solo on the second verse. Do you know the descant?'

'Absolutely,' says Squiffy, and together they sing,

> See the schoolboy a soldier in khaki,
> Changed his bat for the Gatling and Bren.
> How his officer's uniform suits him,
> How much better he speaks than his men.
> Thank the school for his noble demeanour,
> And his poise where vulgarity's rife,
> Knowing always that life is like cricket,
> Not forgetting that cricket's like life.

All right, Son. Obvious question is, how do I know all that? How do I know all that detail about Squiffy Yoxborough?

Answer is, he told me. And he'll tell me again every blooming night if he gets the chance.

Yes, he's inside here with me.

And why? Why did he get caught? Was it because the duke woke up next morning and immediately realised it was a transparent con? Realised that he'd been pissed the night before and that it really was a bit unusual to give a complete stranger a cheque for half a million quid?

No, duke's mind didn't work like that. So long as he thought he was dealing with a genuine Old Raspurian, he reckoned he'd got a good deal. OK, it'd cost him five hundred grand, but, as a price for covering up everything that his son'd done in the past, it was peanuts. The Family Name would remain untarnished – that was the important thing.

But, like I just said, that was only going to work, *so long as he thought he was dealing with a genuine Old Raspurian.*

And something the butler told him the next morning stopped him thinking that he was.

So, when Squiffy goes to the bank to pay in his cheque to the 'Only Real Granite House-Building Construction Techniques' account, he's asked to wait for a minute, and suddenly the cops are all over the shop.

So what was it? He got the voice right, he got the clothes right, he got all the Old Raspurian stuff right, he used the right knives and forks at dinner, he said 'Absolutely' instead of 'Yes' . . . where'd he go wrong?

I'll tell you – when he got up the next morning he made his own bed.

Well, butler sussed him straight away. Poor old Squiffy'd shown up his upbringing. Never occur to the sort of person he was pretending to be to make a bed. There was always servants around to do that for you.

See, there's some things you can learn from outside, and some you got to know from inside. And that making the bed thing, it takes generations of treating peasants like dirt to understand that.

I hope I've made my point. Stick at it, Son. Both the work and the social bit. You're going to get right to the top, like I said. You're not going to be an old-fashioned villain, you're going to do it through the system. And if you're going to succeed, you can't afford the risk of being let down by the sort of mistake that shopped Squiffy Yoxborough. Got that?

Once again, sorry about the Fourth of June. (Mind you, someone else is going to be even sorrier.) I'll see to it you get better parents for the Eton and Harrow Match.

This letter, with the customary greasy oncers, will go out through Blue Phil, as per usual. Look after yourself, Son, and remember – keep a straight bat.

Your loving father,
NOBBY CHESTERFIELD

URBAN LEGEND

Reginald Hill

This is Anne Hardcastle's story and it's a true story, not one of those urban legend things which, according to her, never really happened to anybody. This really happened to Anne. Definitely. I'd stake my life on it. We were very close at the time.

How she knew so much about these legends was she'd spend eighteen months doing research on them so she'd get an MA or something. She had this notebook full of stories. A lot of them I heard before, like the one where this chap accidentally leaves his wife in a lay-by in her nighty, or the one where this chap's granny dies on a touring holiday and the car gets stolen, though I think my favourite's the one about the young married couple next door who like playing Spiderman!

Anyway, Anne had finished her research and come to stay at this old inn at Ludlow to write it up, and one lunchtime she was sitting in the bar when this girl at the next table started telling a story, and Anne's ears pricked because she guessed from the way the girl started, it was going to be one of these urban legends.

'It happened up near Church Stretton on Sunday,' said the girl. 'I heard it last night from my cousin Jenny who works in the tourist office in Shrewsbury, and her boyfriend works in the same accountancy firm as Colin.'

'Who's Colin?' asked someone.

'Shut up and I'll tell you. There was this christening party, see, and when they went to church, someone had to stay behind to see to the smoked salmon and champers, and Avril, the youngest daughter, volunteered. She was a bit of a reb, evidently; worked in London and disapproved of christenings; so she didn't mind missing church.

Now this Colin had always fancied her, only she couldn't stand him, so she wasn't too pleased when he said he'd stay too. In fact she told her sister, any funny stuff and she'd be off back to London like a shot!

'Now according to Colin, fifteen minutes after the christening party left, this chap appeared saying he was a cop and there'd been an accident and her parents were on their way to hospital in Shrewsbury. Naturally Avril jumped straight in her car, but the cop made her move over saying he'd better drive, she was in such a state. And Colin got in too, though he said the cop didn't seem too keen.

'Off they went. It's a maze of little roads round there, but suddenly Colin realised they weren't even on one of these but belting along a rutted cart-track. He asked where the hell they were and the cop said a shortcut, but next thing they ran into this stream across the track where there was a ford for cattle, only the car didn't make it but stalled in the middle.

'They couldn't get it started and Avril was getting really upset, so the cop suggested Colin went for help while he dried the plugs. Downstream they could just glimpse the parapet of a humpback bridge and Colin set off along the bank. It was hard going, all overgrown with brambles and willows, and after a while he paused and glanced back. The cop was under the bonnet, and Avril was walking along the bank upstream. Colin could see a clearing there, and right at the water's edge was this old oak stump all overgrown with ivy, like an altar cloth he said. On the stump someone had stood this sledge-hammer with its long shiny shaft sticking straight up in the air, like Excalibur, he said. And as he watched, Avril sat down on the stump with her head between her hands.

'Finally Colin reached the bridge only to find the road wasn't much better than a track. He scrambled on to the parapet to try to spot a house, but couldn't see anything but woodland. Then suddenly this noise rang out, like a hammer driving a stake into the ground, echoing like thunder so he couldn't tell where it came from.

'Then he glanced down into the stream. And he saw that the water was running red.

'Without thinking, he jumped straight down and started scrambling back upstream like a mad thing. He'd hurt his ankle when he landed, and the willows seemed to be crowding even

closer together, and long before he got there, he realised the
hammering had stopped and the water was running clear once
more.

'And when at last he reached the ford, the car was gone, and
the policeman and Avril, and the sledge-hammer had vanished
from the old oak stump.

'He doesn't know how he got back, but an hour later he came
stumbling out of the coppice at the bottom of the garden. On the
lawn the christening party were standing around with champagne
glasses, but no one was drinking. They were all looking towards
the patio where two uniformed policemen were talking to Avril's
parents, and when Colin tried to join them, the other guests held
him back and told him the police had come with dreadful news.
Avril's car had run off the road this side of Worcester, flipped over
down an embankment, and burnt out with her inside.'

The girl paused for effect.

'My God!' said someone. 'But what did they do when Colin told
his story?'

'Advised him to see his doctor! Everyone reckoned he'd tried it
on with Avril, so she'd just taken off like she'd threatened, and
Colin felt so guilty, he'd say anything to shift the blame. Also one
of the policemen reckoned he'd heard the story before. But Colin
was still telling it yesterday when Jenny's boyfriend rang to see
why he'd stayed off work.'

At the next table Anne was so excited she could hardly breathe.
Evidently the impossible thing with these urban legends is to track
them back to where they started. But with this one, it was different. You see, she reckoned she'd actually invented the original
version of this christening party legend and had been telling it
round the Midlands for eighteen months! The idea was, if ever she
heard it from someone else, she'd be able to backtrack it to herself
with all its variations and she reckoned if she could pull it off, it
would really make her name.

So, first stop was Shrewsbury!

To start with, it was easy. She boxed clever with Jenny in the
tourist office, letting on she was a big mate of the cousin in
Ludlow, and ten minutes later she was at the accountants where
Jenny's boyfriend, George, worked. This was where she expected

the first hiccup, with George saying, 'Actually, it was this friend in another office it happened to . . .'

But George took her by surprise. First he said he was rushed off his feet because he was having to do bloody Stark's work. Then he scribbled an address and handed it to her, saying, 'If you can get the silly sod to snap out of it and get back here I'd be most grateful.'

'I don't follow,' said Anne. 'Whose address is this?'

'Stark's of course. Colin Stark. 'Bye!'

Poor Anne was completely bewildered, but one thing she didn't lack was determination. The address was in Church Stretton. She got in her car and headed south.

It turned out to be a little cottage just outside the village, and as Anne approached, she met an ambulance and a police car belting north. She could still hear their sirens fading as she knocked at Colin Stark's door.

And that was where we met for the first time. I came round the side of the cottage and stood watching her for quite a while before she spotted me. Then she jumped and said, all breathless, 'Mr Stark? Colin Stark?'

I said, no, I wasn't, but why did she want to see Mr Stark? And she said, private business, and who was I anyway?

That's when I introduced myself.

'Detective Constable Brice, miss. Shropshire CID. So you don't actually know Mr Stark?'

'No. Why are you here?'

'There's been a bit of a tragedy, miss,' I said, watching her closely. 'You see, young Mr Stark's been found dead. Suicide it looks like. He's hanged himself.'

For a moment I thought she was going to faint and I grabbed her arm.

'I'm sorry,' I said. 'I wouldn't have come out with it like that only I thought as you didn't know him . . .'

'I'm all right,' she said. 'Oh God, this is terrible. Do you know why . . .?'

'Some girl he knew got killed in an accident and I gather he took it hard.'

That did it. Now, it all came pouring out, all this stuff about urban legends and how she'd made this one up so it couldn't really have happened, and how she wasn't going to rest till she got to the bottom of it . . .

'Whoa!' I said finally. 'Look, miss, this all sounds so way-out, I think you ought to talk to my inspector direct.'

'Fine,' she said. 'Let's go find him.'

She headed back to her car. I offered to drive as she was a bit upset, but she wasn't having that, so I got in the passenger seat. Off we went, with me giving directions and Anne still talking away ten to the dozen. I reckon I got a potted version of most of her research in the next ten minutes but I still must have looked dubious for she dug out her notebook and handed it over, saying, 'It's right at the back, under the Christening Party.'

She was right. There it was, and it certainly had the general outline.

'See what I mean?' she said triumphantly. 'Either it's some crazy coincidence or some madman really did hammer a stake into that poor girl, then faked the car crash and fire . . .'

'Turn left here,' I interrupted.

She obeyed, still talking. ' . . . and in that case, you really ought to be searching for this ford, there must be some traces . . . where are we going?'

At last she'd noticed we were off the road and bumping down a green and rutted track.

'To see my inspector,' I reassured her. 'We've found the ford already and he's down here now, conducting a search.'

I don't think she was convinced but you're ready to believe anything when the alternative's so unbelievable, aren't you? I think she knew when we reached the ford and I switched off the engine and the quiet came rushing in and there wasn't another soul in sight. But she didn't scream, not even when her head slowly turned and she looked upstream into the clearing where the slanting sun fell like a spotlight on the old oak stump, all draped with ivy like an altar cloth, and the shaft of my sledge-hammer rising from it, like Excalibur.

I kept the notebook. I often thumb through it when I want a laugh. But I've never been convinced that Anne actually invented the Christening Party legend. You see, I got the idea from this really genuine chap in Traffic who swears blind it happened to this mate of his in Birmingham . . .

One thing I am sure of. Anne would have kept burrowing away till she got to the bottom of it.

Definitely.

I staked her life on it.

We were very close at the time.

HAPPY CHRISTMAS

Robert Barnard

'The people I'm sorry for at Christmas are the ones with children,'
said Crespin Fawkes, in a voice that rang round the Waggon of Hay.
'It must be dreadful for them.'

He looked around his little group from the corners of his bright
little eyes, registering their appreciative chuckles. Then he took
another sip of his vodka and tonic.

'Think of it: the noise, the toy trumpets, the crackers and the
computer games! Much more appropriate, one would have thought,
as a celebration of the crucifixion!'

This time the appreciation was more muted. The joke would have
been better if he had left it alone. Crespin never had been able to
leave a good thing alone.

But they had all enjoyed the joke, and like all good jokes it went
home to them. They all, in their way, faced a future when their
Christmasses would be alone. The Waggon of Hay was one of those
pubs where what are today called the sexual minorities tended to
congregate. Several of Crespin's group were old boyfriends of his, or
occasional partners, and most of the ones who weren't were so
because Crespin had very definite ideas about what he fancied and
what he didn't. Then there were Joan and Evelyn, who definitely
had a relationship, but who enjoyed male company; and there was
Patty, whom nobody could quite pin down.

Still, the fact was that they were all, except Crespin, young.
Almost all of them would in fact be going home to families for
Christmas, however much they might profess boredom, reluctance
or irritation. Joan, or Evelyn, would ring home and say, 'Can I bring
my flatmate?' and Mummy would say, 'Of *course*, dear!' The others

would go on their own, probably, bearing sophisticated presents from the Metropolis. For three or four days they would be back in the bosoms of their families, cherished and chaste. When you got to Crespin's age you didn't have a family with a bosom to go back to, but that was something in the future for the rest of them. Crespin had always preferred to keep company with young people.

'You're not going down to your sister, then?' asked Gregory.

'My dears, *no!*' said Crespin, with a theatrical shudder. 'Not after last time. And to be perfectly frank, she didn't ask me. She has Teenage Boys, and the fact is she doesn't trust me with them, though last time I saw them they promised to be both pudgy and spotty, which is something I can't *abide*. And her house and grounds are positively country gentry, which is not *me* at all: you expect to see mummers on Christmas Eve, all madly tugging at their forelocks and talking Thomas Hardy. 'Thank 'ee koindly, squoire' – all that stuff. Oh dear, no. Not even for a twenty-pound turkey with all the trimmings would I betake myself to Priscilla's. I *much* prefer my own company, and *la cuisine chez* Marks and Sparks!'

Once more there was a gratifying laugh. Crespin sat back in his seat, his performance over for a few minutes, as he let the younger ones take over. As their talk about who was going with whom washed over him (Crespin had had a lifetime of who was going with whom, had figured in it as often as not), he let his eye rove around the bar. There were the Chelsea locals – for there was a 'straight' clientele as well – there were the blacks, the lesbians, the kinks and the rough trade – these last all friends of Crespin's.

And there, over by the bar, was a boy by himself. Boy? Young man? Somewhere on the border, Crespin judged him. He was eyeing the company speculatively – listening, absorbing. His shirt, dazzling white, looked as if it had been bought that day, but his cardigan, which he had taken off and draped over his arm, was pure home-knit, his jeans were chain store, and his shoes might have been bought for him by his mother for his last year at school. There was about him an indefinable air of newly-up-from-the-country. As Crespin looked at that face, intently absorbing the ambience of the Waggon of Hay, it suddenly struck him that he'd seen it before, knew it, if only slightly – that somewhere or other he had come across this young man as a child.

The young man's eyes, roving around the bar, suddenly met his, and there seemed to Crespin to come into them a flash of recognition. Then he turned to the landlord and ordered a fresh half of lager. Crespin turned back to his friends. This was the last Saturday before Christmas. He wouldn't see them again for quite a while, and the stimulus of their laughter and admiration would be missed. Crespin did need, more so as he got older, laughter and admiration. As for the young man – well, no doubt an opportunity would present itself. It so often did, Crespin found.

In the event, it wasn't so much opportunity that presented itself as the young man himself – 'on a plate, as it were', as Crespin said wonderingly to him. There was a ring on his doorbell on Christmas Eve, and there on the doormat he stood – dark-haired, thick-eyebrowed, strong-shouldered – altogether . . . capable. Crespin warmed to him at once, to the mere sight of him, and smiled his very friendliest smile.

'I hope you'll excuse my bothering you,' said the young man. 'I saw you in the Waggon the other night, you see – '

'And *I* saw *you*,' said Crespin.

'And I saw you in the street the other day too – you didn't see me – and I followed you here.'

'Flattering,' said Crespin. 'Almost invariably, nowadays, it's the other way round.'

'You see, I think I know you. Met you once or twice, years ago. And your picture's on your sister's piano. The boys are always saying, "That's our uncle, who's in television".'

'So much more distinguished than "who's *on* television". Are you sure that's *all* they say?'

The boy smiled, twisting his mouth.

'"That's our uncle, who's queer and in television".'

'Exactly. Don't bother with the censored version. But this leaves open the question of who *you* are.'

'My father's the gardener. I always used to help him, in the school holidays. That's how I met you.'

By now they were both in the hallway of Crespin's awfully amusing flat, and quite naturally Crespin had removed the boy's duffel coat and taken his inadequate scarf. They understood each other so well that no invitation, no pantomime of reluctance, was necessary. Quite soon the boy was sitting on the sofa, with Crespin in the armchair close beside him, and they were both clutching drinks and talking about anything but what Crespin really wanted to talk about, and the boy's eyes were going everywhere. For all that there were slight traces of the bumpkin about him, Crespin decided at once that he was an awfully noticing boy. There was almost nothing in Crespin's living room that escaped his wandering eye.

'You like it? My little nest, I mean?'

'Yes, awfully. It's not like what I'm used to. Even at your sister's –'

'My *dear*, I should think not! Don't even *men*tion my sister's in the same breath if you want to stay in favour! Of course she has the odd good *piece* – could hardly fail to have in a house as old as that – but everything that she's bought herself has been the purest Home Counties. Now *I* rediscovered the Thirties ten or fifteen years before anyone else. I bought, bought, bought, quite ridiculously cheaply, dear boy. I wouldn't like to tell you what some of the things are worth today.'

As he said it, Crespin noticed on those sturdy country features a gleam come into the eye.

'This Beaton, for example. *Only* a photograph, my dear, but in its original frame, and signed to the subject, who was a *quite* minor poet – well, someone offered me four hundred and fifty only the other day. And I paid ten bob for it, back in the days of Harold Macmillan, in a little shop in East Finchley.'

All the time the boy's eyes were watching, waiting for him to go on to another item. Crespin, characteristically, decided to play with him. He sat down beside him on the sofa.

'But don't let's talk about my little knick-knacks. Let's talk about you. I don't even know your name.'

His name, it turned out, was Stephen Hodge.

At home, he said, things hadn't been 'all that bad', but on the other hand he hadn't got on 'all that well' with his parents. His father had been old-fashioned and heavy-handed, and had insisted on his leaving school at sixteen. 'Don't want you loafing around there for the rest of your life, learning things that won't be no use to you,' he had said. Stephen had wanted to stay on. He was middling at most things, but he had definite talent in certain directions: 'Art and that,' he said. He had wanted to get an education to get away from home, find new horizons, 'meet exciting people,' he said. And he added: 'Get new experiences.'

By now they were in the kitchen, and Crespin was preparing one of his risottos.

'Something light,' he said. 'We want to keep our appetites for tomorrow.'

Over the risotto, Crespin returned to the absorbing topic – absorbing, in fact, to both of them – of his flat, his possessions.

'When we've eaten, dear boy, you shall have a tour of the flat. A personally conducted tour, led by the *chatelain*. Then you can feel truly at home here for the festive season. Where are you living, as a rule?'

'I've got this camp bed at a mate's,' said Stephen, eating hungrily as if he had little desire to save his appetite for the morrow. 'He's away for Christmas.'

'Then we are saving each other from some perfectly ghastly festive days. I shall conduct you round my nest and my things, so that you will know them as you will know me.' He smiled at the boy, who slowed down the pace of his eating. 'I can see that you have an eye for fine things.'

This last was said with a touch of malice, but it went unperceived. The boy said:

'I think I do. But I don't have the training and that. I need someone to show me.'

After Crespin had found some ice-cream in the fridge, which Stephen had wolfed up in a way that suggested the schoolboy that showed through some of his clothes, Crespin put on some coffee and they began that tour of the flat. The eye that Crespin had noticed almost from the beginning went everywhere, and the brain stored every item of information. The living room was thirties, but the rest of the flat was pleasantly crowded with more conventional objects. Often Crespin noticed that Stephen wanted to ask the value of something, but managed to refrain. Sometimes Crespin would give it to him, sometimes not. He began to drop pieces and sale values, but ambiguously ('Would you believe me if I said fifteen hundred?'). He was already playing with his guest – beginning the games that would be conducted more roughly in the bedroom.

Soon a refinement of the game suggested itself to him. Instead of being ambiguous, his assertions of value became downright mendacious. His valuable things – of yes, ducky, he did *have* valuable things – were commended as amusing trifles, no more. The highest commendation, and implied value, were lavished on pieces whose worth was at best sentimental.

If *that*, said Crespin to himself, as he held – gently, as if it were Ming, and he a museum curator – a piece of nondescript china inherited from his Aunt Molly, which looked as if it had been purchased from Woolworths in the twenties.

'*Ex*quisite,' said Crespin. 'And beautifully kept, you notice. Trust my Aunt Molly for that, dragon that she was. I wouldn't like to tell you what my friend Henry at Chez Moi Antiques round the corner would offer me for that, if I ever told him I'd sell.'

He saw the boy, in some space behind his eyes, file the information away. For a moment Crespin felt himself washed by a wave of nausea and ennui. So many young men – tough, capable, greedy. So many nights of delicious brutality, followed by less delicious humiliation, depredation, loss. He shrugged the feeling aside, and went on with the tour. Crespin was a magpie. Only a fraction of his things could be shown that evening. There would be plenty left to talk about the next day.

After coffee, and after all the china and glass had been safely tucked away inside the washing-up machine, the games started again, but this time they were more physical, and this time it was Crespin who was victim. And in these games Stephen understood what was going on. It was amazing how quickly he got the idea. But then, he had been in London some weeks. Crespin had no reason to think he was the first of his kind that the boy had been with. If he frequented the Waggon of Hay, after all . . .

But it was a pleasure to encounter a lad with that sturdiness of physique, yet with that delicate inventiveness of mind. They started with the schoolboy stuff, with the arm twisted behind the back, but then they proceeded, sometimes Crespin suggesting, sometimes Stephen improvising, to more serious brutalities. Half way through the games, both of them sweaty, Crespin a little bloody, they stopped for a neat Scotch. By this time they had very little in the way of clothes on, and some of Crespin's, lying on the floor, were torn and dirty. As he drained his glass Crespin plunged his other hand down Stephen's schoolboyish Y-fronts, and the games began again, until they climaxed, gloriously on the bed, Stephen's big hands around Crespin's throat as he lay on top of him.

'It's been one of the most wonderful nights of my life,' Crespin said, after Stephen had roughly taken him for the second time.

The next morning Crespin was up early, showering away the dried blood, and gazing with satisfaction at the discolouration of his skin as bruises began to show. Before going into the kitchen he went through the lounge and drawing room, looking for something sufficiently masculine to present to Stephen on Our Lord's birthday. He found nothing that satisfied him, and in the end wrapped up a really beautiful Georgian silver cream jug. In his gifts, at least, he would be generous, he thought. He made tea and toast, set out the tray for two, then put the present on the tray and went into the bedroom. Stephen was awake and sitting up. Crespin thought he had never seen anything more beautiful. He sat the tray on the boy's lap, presented him with the little parcel, then sat himself cross-legged on the end of the bed.

'It's beautiful, really beautiful,' Stephen said, gazing at the silver object.

'Nothing – a mere nothing,' said Crespin, with his characteristic wave of the hand.

'And I have nothing to give you.'

'Do you imagine you could give me anything more wonderful than you have given me already?' asked Crespin. Stephen looked pleased, and Crespin added: 'Dear boy . . .'

They had a quiet morning preparing the lunch. The cookery of Mrs Marks and Mrs Spencer did not need long in the oven – Crespin was pleased to find that he had two packets of stuffed turkey breast in the deep freeze. He would feed Stephen up. He knew the boy was hungrier than, so far, he had been able to satisfy. He peeled a mountain of potatoes and carrots, set out the cranberry sauce on a pretty Meissen dish, opened the tin of National Trust Christmas pudding. Stephen's eyes sparkled at this: he still had a child's love of sweet things. While this was going on, Stephen did his bit around the place, clearing up from the night before and setting the table, at which he proved surprisingly adept. In between they watched bits of the Christmas morning service on television.

'Are you religious?' asked Stephen.

'I converted to Rome when I was eighteen,' said Crespin, with some signs of pride. 'Inevitably, with my name, I suppose. Such a relief after the middle-of-the-road Anglicanism of my childhood – the middle-of-the-road down which my dear sister and her family still happily plod. But somehow the conversion didn't last. I regret it. And you?'

'I don't know. I don't go to church and that. But sometimes I watch it on television and it seems to . . . have something. But I'm not religious. It doesn't sort of . . . go, does it?'

'Go?'

'With us. With the sort of lives we lead.'

'No,' agreed Crespin sadly. Soon he went back to the kitchen.

They ate about two o'clock. The meal was a great success. Stephen ate about two-thirds of the turkey, and was clearly pleased with a Christmas dinner that was all breast and no leg or wing. He made significant inroads into the vegetables, and seemed to enjoy Crespin's cream on the Christmas pudding in place of the custard he always had at home. Before the meal they had a glass of sherry – Reina Victoria. Stephen said it was like no sherry he had ever had before, inspected the bottle and asked how much it cost. As they ate Crespin gave him his little lecture on moselle. How often had he given it before, over dinner, to a bored, contemptuous or frankly dim-witted companion? Stephen followed him, asked questions, stored up the answers.

He will take everything I have to give him, thought Crespin.

'Do you want to ring your family?' he asked.

'No,' said Stephen awkwardly. 'No. They don't know where I am, you see.'

'I'm not pressing you. That's your business.'

'Will you be ringing your sister? Don't say anything if so.'

'I shan't ring her. She won't be expecting it. Nobody will. Outside my job I have nobody.' Crespin paused, then said deliberately: 'I could lie here, dead, for days, weeks, and nobody would know . . .'

He registered, unmistakably, a tiny glint in the boy's eye.

They went back to the living room for coffee, and as he poured it and handed his to Stephen, Crespin said: 'This has been a Christmas to remember.'

'For me too,' said Stephen.

'Two days, wonderfully marked off from the humdrum round.'

'Maybe we could do it again.'

'Dear boy, *repetition*, even if it were possible, is not advisable. Exquisite pleasure is a one-off thing. With your inventive mind you should understand that.'

Stephen smiled slowly.

'You think I have an inventive mind?'

'I know you have. I'm in a position to pronounce on the subject.'

Stephen stirred his coffee.

'I could stay.'

'Dear boy!' cried Crespin, fluttering his hand. 'Do you imagine I could stand excitements like last night's every day?'

'We wouldn't need to go at it like that every day.'

'If you were here, *with* me, how could we not? Come, you've never seen my study. Let me continue with your aesthetic education.'

So Crespin resumed yesterday's game, with renewed zest. He had the boy at an ideal stage: he was quick but ignorant. In a year's time – if he remained at large – this particular fun would no longer be possible. He would *know*. Now he was anxious to learn, but did not know. Thus Crespin could wave aside a rare, intimate conversation piece by John Singer Sargent which hung over the mantelpiece as, 'A mere daub, dear boy. Hardly worth the canvas and oil. Though I keep it for sentimental reasons.'

He paused, as an idea seemed to strike him. He looked up at the stalwart man, the worried wife, and the three girls of the picture.

'My great-grandfather, the Admiral. And his three jolly-tar daughters. Imagine – that his blood should have diluted itself into mine. Funnily enough, I remember one of the daughters, in old age, chivvying me into manly sports. The Admiral, I always suspect, would have gone in for more drastic remedies. Probably have had me drowned at birth. He was never one for half-measures.'

Crespin, watched by the boy, tore his eyes from the exquisite 'daub' over the fireplace and took, very casually, from on top of a bureau a large, silver-encrusted nineteenth-century firearm.

'This was his. Isn't it handsome? And characteristically assertive. Feel the weight of it.'

The boy took it, and in his surprise nearly dropped it. It was as heavy as Death.

'It's not a gun at all, in fact. Really more of a cudgel. He had it made to his own specifications. He always said that if you shot an intruder some damn fool was going to ask questions. With this you could either terrify him or bash the daylights out of him if it didn't work.' Crespin looked at Stephen, and took the weapon from his hands. 'It's one of the best pieces I own. I always think it might come in useful some day, to somebody.'

Their glance at each other held a brief flash of understanding. Then they went on to other things. As before Crespin praised cut-glass vases and commercial prints as if they were priceless objects the Victoria and Albert were itching to get their hands on. The pleasure was redoubled because, in addition to observing that pricing-and-cataloguing routine going on behind the boy's eyes, he had a sense of something more, too: of the boy screwing himself up to something. When he put his hand on his arm, or delicately round his waist, he could feel it was already manifesting itself physically in a bodily tenseness.

Those brief touches, those affectionate squeezes, inevitably began to lead to something more, but Crespin was not anxious to start on the serious business yet. He wanted a cup of tea. He had always enjoyed tea, and served it in a ceremonious way that reminded him of his mother. He would enjoy one more cup.

The boy's tensions had relaxed by the time they both drank tea. For a moment Crespin wondered whether he had changed his mind, but he was reassured to notice a tiny smile of anticipation playing around his lips: he was relaxed because he had decided to do it.

Conversation between them was strained and spasmodic, as it had never been since Stephen had arrived. Now they had between them an unspoken contract. Any mention of it could only render it ludicrous and void. So they must talk about other things, though other things scarcely came. At last Crespin put an end to it after one cup. Second cups were always less than perfect. He turned towards the boy beside him on the sofa, and began gently to unbutton his shirt. Stephen, at least, must look kempt when he left the flat.

His own clothes were another matter. God knew, he had not exactly been cautious in the past. Now there was nothing he wore that could mean anything to him again. But as the game hotted up, no item was given up without a struggle. The shirt went as he was held back forcefully over the sofa, his head being pummelled by one fist as the boy's other hand tore at the flaunting pink silk. Other items went as they fought across the table, chased each other round the kitchen, sank into violent clinches on to the floor. There were intervals of something like tenderness, almost peace, as their naked bodies came together in something other than struggle. There was a moment, on the rug, in front of the gas fire, when it almost seemed as if the contract between them might be forgotten. It was Crespin who ended it. He slapped Stephen ineffectually across the cheeks.

'Pig!' he shouted. 'Yokel! Rustic yob!'

Stephen's fists began brutally hitting him about the head, first left, then right, leaving Crespin breathless. Then Stephen unclenched his hands and felt for the throat. It was a feeling that had always excited Crespin, but he knew that this time he could not give way to his excitement. That was not the way he had to go. It had to be by the Admiral's gun. He writhed on the rug, twisted and turned within those strong hands. The bodies came together, then slid off one another, until suddenly Crespin managed to knee the boy in the groin. With a wrench he struggled away as Stephen let go his hands, then he ran for the bedroom.

'Come for me!' he shouted. 'Come for me!'

He slammed the door, but it swung open again. He stood there in the darkness, panting, aching, watching the light from the living room as it filtered through the opening in the doorway. The boy was not coming. Wait. He heard a floorboard creak. The one just inside the study door. He was going for the weapon. Perhaps he was looking round – at the things he would take, the things he had marked off in his little inventory, the things that would fetch the odd pound merely when he hawked them round the antique shops, as soon as he dared.

Crespin's breath was coming more easily now. Let him come! Let him not break the rhythm! He heard the floorboard creak again. He heard soft footsteps across the carpeted floor of the living room. He was coming after all. The game would be played through.

And as he saw, in the lighted doorway of the bedroom, a large, dark shadow, there flooded over him an overwhelming feeling of excitement and fulfilment. It had been the happiest Christmas of his adult life.

BAD MOVE

Herbert Harris

The villagers of Nether Wickstead will all tell you that the nearest thing to Miss Marple – Agatha Christie's elderly lady sleuth – is Miss Amelia Wadsworth, retired headmistress of St Martin's Girls' School.

Miss Wadsworth is possessed of a keen observation, a retentive memory, and an inquiring mind, qualities which (like Miss Marple's) have sometimes proved useful to the constabulary of Nether Wickstead and its neighbouring villages.

It was her inquiring mind which made her ask herself one day during the summer: 'Why hasn't Constance invited me this year to the Littlebourne Horticultural Society's Summer Show?'

Why indeed? Miss Wadsworth and Mrs Constance Lovelace had been close friends for many years, sisters under the skin, or under the topsoil, as far as horticulture is concerned.

The latter, in fact, had been a moving spirit behind the Littlebourne Horticultural Society, and at their Spring Show she had said very clearly: 'Amelia, you *must* come to our Summer Show! I shall make a special point of telephoning and reminding you nearer the date!'

Only Mrs Lovelace hadn't, and that was what caused her old friend some concern. It was some time since Constance had been in touch.

When Miss Wadsworth paid a visit to the neighbouring village of Littlebourne, having failed to contact her friend by telephone, the first person she met on alighting from the bus was George Burton, who ran a small nursery and had been Mrs Lovelace's right-hand man in staging the local flower shows.

'Didn't you know?' he said in reply to Miss Wadsworth's inquiry. 'Mrs Lovelace suddenly decided to push off to Ozzieland!'

Miss Wadsworth frowned. 'Australia? You mean she's gone there to live?'

'Yes. From what I gather, she's got some relative there who's been badgerin' her to go and settle out there.'

'She never told me anything about that,' Miss Wadsworth said, looking astonished. 'Most extraordinary!'

The nurseryman gave a contemptuous snort. 'Can't say as how I blame her. She's not had much of a life with that good-for-nothing son of hers since her husband Norman died.'

'Oh dear, I never realised,' Miss Wadsworth said sadly. 'I only met her son once. Harry, isn't it? It was in Constance's garden. He did seem a rather unpleasant fellow now you come to mention it. Tried to persuade her to sell her house and move into a flat.'

'Yes, and Mrs Lovelace wouldn't have none of that! She'd have had to give up her garden, and that garden was her life!'

'Indeed, yes,' Miss Wadsworth agreed fervently. 'She had created the garden from nothing. It seems very odd she should run off to Australia and leave it all behind. Like abandoning a child, you might say.'

'My missus used them very words,' George Burton said. 'Well, I 'ope you'll excuse me, Miss Wadsworth, but I've left a tray of seedlings in the hot sun and the poor little perishers will die of thirst if I don't go and give 'em a drink.'

Miss Wadsworth stood for some while thinking after George Burton had left. Then, with a determined look about her mouth, she marched off in the direction of Laburnum Lodge, the home which Constance Lovelace and her late husband Norman had shared for many happy years.

She made her way up the gravel drive of the attractive old house, and the short flight of stone steps leading to the front door, beside which was a bell-push which she pressed firmly. She could hear the ringing of the bell, but nobody came to answer the door. She rang a second time, but still nobody came.

And then, remembering what a beautiful garden Mrs Lovelace had created at the rear of the house, she made her way down a side passage to look at it and admire it as she had done so many times before. On many occasions in the past she had even helped her friend Constance to decide which were the best blooms to enter for the Horticultural Society shows.

She recalled Constance's passion for peonies, and how they would discuss the competing merits of 'Pink Delight' and 'Bower of Roses' and chuckle over their attempts to pronounce 'Mlokosewitschii'. And Constance's fussiness about choosing a site shaded from the early morning sun . . .

It was while Miss Wadsworth was standing staring at an area of the garden at the other end of a long herbaceous border that an elderly grey-haired man suddenly peered across the top of the brick wall.

'Excuse me, madam, but are you looking for somebody?' he asked.

Somewhat startled out of her reverie, Miss Wadsworth gazed up at him. 'Well, yes . . . the present occupant.'

'If you're interested in buying the place, you'll have to see Selby and Mitcham, the agents up in the High Street,' the neighbour informed her.

'Yes, I'll do that,' she said, thinking quickly, 'but I was hoping that I might see Mrs Lovelace's son Harry, whom I know.'

'Ah, well, you won't see *him*, because he lives up in London and he only shows up very rarely.'

Miss Wadsworth sighed and took the plunge. 'It's a pity he didn't visit his mother more often. The way he treated her was dreadful!'

'You can say that again!' the grey-haired man said. 'I'm not surprised she pushed off to Australia. He was always borrowing money from her to pay off his gambling debts or to give one of his blonde floozies a good time.'

'Her departure was very sudden, wasn't it?'

'Very, and she won't be coming back either.'

'She's selling the house then?'

'Well, her son's selling it for her, I gather. Apparently she authorised him to sell the house, invest the money, and arrange for the interest to be sent out to her in Australia.'

'Did she indeed? And did she put that in writing?'

'I suppose she did.'

Miss Wadsworth shook her head. 'Suppositions are always dangerous. There are such things as forgeries.'

'Well, yes, but I'm not quite with you, Mrs . . .'

'Miss,' corrected Miss Wadsworth. 'And I'll tell you something else. I'm going to have a chat with Sergeant Morris at the local police station, whom I also know. You see, I've spotted something that has got me rather worried.'

Sergeant Morris, a rather harassed looking man, expected to devote too much of his time to vandals and louts, glanced up when a constable showed her into his office. 'I know you, don't I?' he said.

'It was two years ago. Somebody stole the silver cups from a flower show marquee out on Blake's Meadow. Very daring. I'm Miss Wadsworth. I told you who did it.'

'So you did,' recalled the sergeant. 'And what are you going to tell me this time?'

'I'm not going to tell you anything at this stage,' answered Miss Wadsworth, 'but I'm going to suggest that an old friend of mine named Constance Lovelace, of Laburnum Lodge, who is alleged to have emigrated to Australia, was possibly murdered by her son Harry.'

'Why?' asked the sergeant.

'To get her money, of course,' said Miss Wadsworth. 'Her house is now worth something like two hundred thousand pounds, and Harry, I would suggest, has devised a nice little scheme to get hold of it.'

Sergeant Morris raised his eyebrows and pursed his lips. 'Is there a body?' he wanted to know.

'I think you will have to dig for that, Sergeant . . . in the herbaceous border.'

'And you know precisely where, I suppose?'

'Yes, I think so,' Miss Wadsworth answered confidently. 'It's where the peonies used to be.'

'The peonies?'

'Yes. You must understand that my friend Constance was a great plantswoman, a most meticulous gardener. A patch of peonies has been moved, you see, and to Constance – a peony specialist, I might add – the idea of moving them, once they were well established, would have been quite unthinkable. You *never* move peonies, Sergeant. And that's where Harry, a non-gardener has, I think, come unstuck.'

'We'd better have a look,' said Sergeant Morris.

They did. And, as usual, Miss Wadsworth was quite right.

SOMETHING TO DECLARE

David Williams

Percy Crickle had been married to Sybil for seventeen years before he
determined to do away with her. The decision was triggered by her
attitude over the winnings. It was the sheer ingratitude that stung
Percy, coming on top of the massive disappointment she had caused
him.

From the very beginning, Percy's mother had insisted he was
marrying beneath him. His late father had been an underpaid
schoolmaster. Sybil's father was a retail grocer whom Mrs Crickle
(Senior) invariably and pointedly referred to as a tradesman. She
described overweight Sybil as a pudding, also as graceless and
untutored. She had never understood what a good-looking boy like
Percy saw in the girl – or woman rather, since Sybil was already
pushing thirty-four at the time of the wedding.

But Percy had been taking the long view. He was then nearly
thirty himself, and still living at home. Nor had he quite settled on a
career – discounting several false starts as a professional trainee. His
mother had put those down to experience, which was inaccurate or,
at best, paradoxical. Meaningful work experience was to elude
Percy throughout his adult life: he partially made up for the lack
with a just-sustaining sort of cunning. He figured that marriage to
Sybil would be bearable, and better than that when she came into
her inheritance.

For her part, God-fearing and trusting Sybil was genuinely in love
with Percy. This was a sentiment quite separate from the incautious
and transitory pleasure she felt about getting a husband well after
the point where she considered marriage a serious prospect.

As for the inheritance, Sybil was a late and only child, with parents who were hard-working, appearing prosperous – and quite old. It had seemed to Percy to be only a matter of time before the fruits of their labours fell to their offspring. When that day arrived he dreamed he would retire from his work – type unspecified – to devote himself to personal improvement of a vaguely academic nature.

In the years following the marriage, it was Sybil who brought in the larger part of their income. She had gone on working in her father's shop which was in a not very affluent part of Liverpool. Percy meantime elected to become a salesman, though with small success. But career set-backs never seriously perturbed him: after all he was only marking time. There were no children of the marriage.

After sixteen years, Sybil's father died suddenly. Then it was revealed that the grocery business had been on the brink of bankruptcy for some time. Sybil's mother sold the shop, exchanging the modest sum it fetched for a life annuity. So it was doubly unfortunate that she also died soon after: the annuity died with her. That was the end of Sybil's expectancy.

Since it was the prospect of the retail fortune that had kept Percy going, its failure to materialise upset him severely: the year that followed was the most depressing in his life. It burned in him too that Sybil continued to earn considerably more than he did. She had become chief check-out assistant in a supermarket.

But it was the sense of injustice that hurt Percy most – and he made no bones about that. He no longer bothered to conceal from Sybil that he had married her for her father's money, now that it was clear her father had had no money.

It was no good Sybil reminding Percy that her father's engagement present to her had been the house they still lived in. Percy had now taken to denouncing that very act of benevolence as a mere stratagem, alleging bizarrely that if her scheming father had not provided a roof for her, Sybil would probably by now have been living in a hostel for aging spinsters.

There had really been no end to Percy's calculated unkindnesses. They made Sybil very sad and dejected, and this prompted her to eat more, so that she became even fatter than before. But if she had been disillusioned about the reason for her marriage, and left in no doubt about why it survived at all (the house being in her name, Percy had nowhere else to live), Sybil's love for her husband still miraculously endured. If she was miserable in herself, in charity, she was also deeply sorry for Percy whose values she now realised had always been horribly distorted. She prayed over that.

Sybil had never let on that she risked a modest stake on the football pools each week. So it came as nothing less than a miracle to Percy when she quietly announced one day that she had won a first dividend – a fraction over £300,000. The sum far exceeded what Percy had expected Sybil might have inherited from her father. He was overjoyed, magnanimously allowing that her past failure to meet his financial goals could now be overlooked. He also made arrangements to quit his latest job as a local government clerk – too early, as it proved.

If Percy's attitude to Sybil had altered, so had hers toward him. Now she was in the ascendant position she determined to stay there, while striving to put some goodness, unselfishness and a right balance into his nature. To begin with, instead of depositing her winnings in their joint bank account, she opened a new account with it in her sole name at a quite different bank. She refused also to consider moving to a larger house, to relinquish her job, or to fund any drastic change in their style of living. She did give Percy a small weekly allowance – but only so long as he stayed in work. The regular donations she started making to deserving charities she explained were uplifting thank-offerings on behalf of both of them.

Far from being uplifted, Percy came to feel even more cheated than before, though this time he hesitated to say as much. And no amount of gentle persuasion on his part would alter Sybil's attitudes. He even started to accompany her to church, something he had never done before and which he did now only to show how his values had changed. Certainly this did impress his wife, and increased her trust in him.

But Sybil continued to insist that the new money would be needed to protect them in their old age: she remained oblivious to Percy's plea that there was enough to cover middle age as well, starting immediately. Sybil had her own reasons for cautioning him that some day one of them would be left to survive alone – possibly to a very great age. There she had made a mistake, for it was thinking about that very thing that put homicide into Percy's mind.

Sybil's other mistake was her one significant concession. She determined to indulge a lifelong aspiration by taking a cruise. After a great deal of searching through brochures she settled on a two-week, late spring voyage in the Bay of Bengal, because it was cheaper than most others, and because she had always wanted to see India and Burma. Percy was welcome to go with her if he wished, although since he distrusted foreigners and loathed foreign countries, as an alternative she offered to pay for him to spend the same period at a three-star hotel in Torquay, a resort he had always favoured.

Percy chose the cruise with an avidity he had difficulty in disguising, but disguise it he did to avoid giving rise to suspicion. Although he detested 'abroad', at the first suggestion of the trip, the possibility of arranging an accidental death at sea positively leapt into the forefront of his mind, where it remained until he turned possibility into fact. Torquay could wait.

They flew from London to Sri Lanka to join the cruise ship in Colombo. It was Polish-owned, middle-sized and middle-aged. Its four week total itinerary took in ports around the Bay of Bengal, then Malaysia, Singapore, Borneo, and Java before it returned via the western coast of Sumatra. Passengers could engage for half the cruise, as Percy and Sybil were doing, joining or leaving the ship in Sri Lanka or Malaysia.

The two were given an outside cabin on the second deck near the centre, and close to the stairs to the upper deck where the restaurant and bar were located. Above the upper deck was the boat deck, for open-air promenading, with a swimming pool aft. Although their cabin had a porthole, Percy early determined with reluctance that it was too small to squeeze fat Sybil through, kicking or otherwise.

In the restaurant they were obliged permanently to share a table for four. The limited number of smaller tables was reserved for passengers taking the whole cruise. Their two female table companions were also the occupants of one of the cabins next door to their own: this was one of the earliest disclosures during the polite exchanges at the first meal.

The women, Kirsty Redley, a widow, and her unmarried younger sister, Rita Stork, were a vivacious pair of slim and attractive if somewhat brassy blondes. They both looked to be under thirty and were altogether a contrast to the other passengers who, in the main, were much older and decidedly staider. Indeed, people wondered what two such youthful, glamorous spirits were doing on such a predictably unexciting cruise. If they were here in hopes of making new men friends the girls must have been disappointed: the few disengaged males aboard were very old indeed. In consequence, the more perceptive wives kept watchful eyes on their husbands when Mrs Redley and Miss Stork were close. This applied especially in the case of Rita Stork, a competent and seemingly ever present amateur photographer, whose obsession with taking candid camera shots was not always appreciated by her subjects. She snapped the Crickles more often than others – perhaps because Sybil seemed to enjoy the experience.

Certainly tolerant Sybil did not regard the girls as predators. As for Percy, while accepting that his late mother would unquestionably have described Kirsty and Rita as common, he was delighted at being thrown with them so regularly, even if their frank conversation and sometimes their behaviour struck him as daring. If he had not had a more burning issue on his mind, he would certainly have responded to what he took to be Rita's occasional explorative advances under the table.

As it was, though, Percy was applying himself wholly to creating the perfect opportunity for pushing Sybil overboard – an exercise that was proving more difficult than he had expected. The deed could certainly not be done in daylight, nor from a place where her fall was likely to be seen or her cries heard. It also needed to be at a time when Sybil's absence would not cause immediate alarm. Above all, the circumstances had to be such that no blame or suspicion could be levelled at Percy.

Their time aboard was over half completed before Percy was satisfied that he had a usable plan. Even then he was to depend on the right weather conditions, and fearful that they might never occur.

Encouraged by her husband, every night after dinner Sybil took a turn around the boat deck in Percy's company. Since the nights were often quite cool, most of the few passengers who liked to walk at this time did so on the closed main deck, which also saved them from having to climb another flight of steps. After their exercise, Percy would escort Sybil to their cabin. Then he would ring for a pot of tea to be sent along to her before he returned to the main deck lounge to play bridge with a group of regulars. Sybil did not care for card games, and in any case she liked to go to bed early with a book.

The duty steward usually brought the tea promptly. If over-modest Sybil was still undressing when he knocked, she would call to him to leave the tray outside. Percy knew this because on one night it happened he was in the bathroom when she had done so – and on a subsequent night when he had purposely locked himself in there, at once to check that she would do so again, as well as to make an important preparation.

It was in the Andaman Sea that Percy pushed Sybil over. The ship was just out of Rangoon on the three day run to Port Kelang in Malaysia, where the Crickles were due to disembark. As they finished dinner a bout of heavy rain had just eased off. The night was uninviting – not cold, but dank and overcast. Altogether the conditions were perfect for Percy's plan.

Sybil took some persuading to come to the open deck which was otherwise predictably empty, but she did so to please Percy, even though she had been feeling unwell. When Percy paused to look over the side, just behind the davit of the aftermost lifeboat, Sybil paused with him.

There was no one else in view. The lifeboat prevented the couple from being seen by the look-out on the bridge deck, just as the same object shaded them somewhat from the general illumination. Percy had planned their position carefully.

'See the flying fish?' he questioned eagerly.

As Sybil leaned across the rail, squinting with enthusiasm, he stepped behind her, grasped both her ankles and heaved her into eternity.

The splash she made hardly registered in the rush of water along the ship's side. Her cry was lost in the churning made by the port screw close to where she went in. Any further sign of her was lost in the immediate tumult of the ship's wake, and then in the murk and darkness.

Sybil died quickly – of shock not drowning. The metabolic imbalance that caused her obesity had long put her heart and life at risk. She had been taking treatment without telling Percy, while doing her best to teach him how to fend for himself without her.

Afterwhat had been at once the most frightening as well as the most despicable act of his whole worthless life, Percy finished his promenade alone. For the time being the balance of his mind was sustained by what he urged himself to regard as the justice of his cause. It happened he met no one as he went down to the cabin at around the usual time, but an encounter would still not have troubled him.

Sybil had complained of feeling off-colour at lunch and dinner. She had mentioned it to several people. The cause was the cold-cure capsule that Percy had surreptitiously dissolved in her early morning tea, after he heard the weather forecast: cold cures upset her. If anyone had asked, her indisposition would explain why she had returned to their cabin ahead of Percy. He had rung for her tea as usual.

When the steward knocked, Percy had played the tape he had made in the bathroom of Sybil's shrill :'Oh, leave it outside please . . . Thank you . . . Good night.'

But before the man could do as instructed, Percy had opened the door. 'OK, I'll take it.' He had placed the tray just inside the cabin, as he called in the direction of the bathroom, 'Sleep well, darling. I won't be late.' Then he had stepped into the corridor and closed the cabin door. 'My wife isn't feeling well,' he had remarked to the steward as they moved together in the direction of the stairs. 'Needs sleep, that's all. Keep an ear open in case she phones though, would you? If she should need me I'll be in the main lounge playing bridge.'

'Very good, sir,' the Pole had replied, gratefully pocketing the over-large tip which had been intended to mark events clearly in his mind.

Two hours later Percy looked up from his cards to glance at the time. 'Oh Lord, I promised to look in on my wife before now.'

'I'll go,' said his partner, the normally reticent Miss Mold, understood to be a retired nurse. She was dummy for the hand. 'I need to freshen up anyway. Give me your key.'

He had been relying on her to volunteer: her cabin was close to his. He had mentioned earlier that Sybil had not been feeling up to scratch.

Miss Mold returned shortly to report that Sybil was not in the cabin, that her bed had not been used, and that the contents of a sleeping pill bottle had been spilled on to the counterpane.

Percy affected puzzlement, not alarm. 'That's strange,' he said. 'Perhaps she found it too hot in the cabin. Or felt better, and went for a walk. D'you think I should go and look for her?'

'Who's lost? Not Sybil?' It was Rita Stork's voice. She had come up behind Miss Mold. 'I'm not sure, but I think I saw her going up to the boat deck. That was about an hour ago. She was ever so groggy at dinner.'

Percy found Rita's mistaken observation almost too good to be true. Now with a deeply concerned expression he asked to be excused from the game to look for his wife. Rita and Miss Mold went with him. After they had searched both promenade decks, the cinema and games rooms on the third deck, and checked the cabin frequently, it was Rita who suggested they should tell the Purser.

In another hour the Captain reluctantly decided to turn the ship about. By then the crew and most of the passengers had been engaged in a meticulous search for Sybil who had failed to respond to repeated summonses over the broadcasting system. A now distracted Percy was plied with the professional ministrations of Miss Mold and the warmly feminine ones of Rita Stork.

Sybil's body was never found, although the sea search went on well into the following afternoon with other ships in the vicinity assisting. Everyone agreed with the Captain's verdict – that sick Sybil had gone for a walk on the open deck and, fuddled by phenobarbitone, had fallen overboard. It seemed to be the only explanation.

People were deeply sympathetic to Percy, especially Rita, her sister Kirsty and quiet Miss Mold. He stayed in his cabin for almost the remainder of the voyage, appearing only once for a meal, and affecting then to be completely broken.

Late on their last night at sea, Rita came to see him from next door – to make sure that he was all right, she explained. It was nearly midnight, and after most people had retired. He was in bed already, reading a girlie magazine which he quickly hid at Rita's knock. He also adopted his bereft expression for her benefit, while not being able to resist stealing lascivious glances at her when he thought she wasn't looking. She was wearing a frilly négligé loosely fastened over a low-cut, diaphanous nightie.

After making a show of tidying the cabin, Rita poured a whisky

and took it to Percy. 'Drink it. It'll do you good. Help you sleep,'
she said. Her fingers stayed on his as he took the glass. 'Now is there
anything else you need? Anything at all?' She sat on the bed and
crossed her legs, allowing the négligé to fall open completely.

'You could . . . you could kiss me goodnight,' he half stammered,
hoping it sounded like an innocent request for further harmless
consolation.

'Oh, you poor man. And I'd like that, Percy love,' she answered.
'I'd like that very much. So let's do it properly, shall we?' She stood
up, letting the négligé fall from her. Then she opened the
bedclothes and slipped in beside him.

The following day was to be an unnerving one for Percy.

Because of the delay in searching for Sybil, the ship arrived at
Port Kelang well behind schedule and too late for departing
passengers to reach Kuala Lumpur in time to catch their flight to
London. Since the ship had to leave almost immediately, the
passengers were sent by train to the Malaysian capital, to spend an
extra night there, in an hotel, at the shipping company's expense.

There clearly being no purpose in Percy keeping Sybil's clothes,
before leaving the ship he gave most of them to a stewardess who was
more or less Sybil's size. As far as he remembered later, it was he who
had suggested Rita and Kirsty should each choose a keepsake from
Sybil's other things, in gratitude for the comfort they had given him –
publicly and otherwise. Rita had chosen the bright red cashmere wrap
Sybil had bought in Madras and had afterwards worn so frequently.
Kirsty had selected a chunky and distinctive necklace.

After the short train journey, Percy had reported as instructed to
the British High Commissioner's Office. He was there for some
hours giving a detailed account of the tragedy. In addition he had
to go over the Captain's and the Deck Officer's reports which
arrived from the Polish Embassy after some delay, and then had to
be translated, along with a deposition from the steward who was
the last person Sybil was known to have spoken to before her death.
In the English version, at least, the steward's statement implied
that he had seen Sybil as well as heard her: Percy was glad to
confirm that this had been the case, confident that the man was
not likely to be available again to correct him.

The First Secretary who dealt with Percy was earnest, sympathetic, unconcerned with time, and quite unruffled that Sybil, a British citizen, had met her end while under Polish jurisdiction, in Burmese waters, with the case now to be cleared in conformity with Malaysian law. It seemed there were well-tried procedures to meet these complicated circumstances: only those procedures had to be observed exhaustively.

The matter seemed to be concluded at the point where Percy gravely signed a form stating that should Sybil's remains ever come to light he authorised that they should be reverently and promptly returned to Britain. His pen had hesitated over the choice of whether his wife's remains should in that event be despatched by air or by sea: in the end he opted for air as showing greater keenness on his part. He was thereafter free to go home next day. And free was the operative word.

'Would you like me to take you to the airport in the morning?' asked the First Secretary as they were about to part. 'I'll be glad to. Get you diplomatic cover through customs and so on. After what you've been through you deserve to be spared all that.'

'No thanks. I'll be fine on my own, really,' Percy answered, anxious above all to get beyond the reach of serious officialdom. Customs would be no problem.

'Very well. As part of a cruise group in transit you shouldn't really have any trouble,' were the diplomat's last words.

What had come after Sybil's murder had drained Percy much more than the act itself. Even the unexpected love-making with Rita had been the less enjoyed because of his deteriorating nervous condition. Now he just wanted to be left alone with nothing to worry about – and the thick end of £300,000 waiting for him to enjoy.

He was sorry not to see Rita again that night, but he understood why. The sisters had told him they would be out for the evening. It was after ten o'clock when he got to the hotel. Before going to bed he took coffee with the ever solicitous Miss Mold. This was hardly a substitute for Rita's amorous attentions, but it was good for appearances sake. It still would not do for him to be seen too much in the company of nubile, younger females. Rita had seriously advised as much before she had left him the night before.

'Well you can't be in mourning for ever, can you, love? It's not natural. Wouldn't bring Sybil back either,' she had said while snuggling close to him. 'But you know how people are. You don't want this lot thinking you're cutting loose too early. Different when we get home,' she had ended, the words heavy with promise as she traced a finger over his lips.

It was why he had kept his distance from the sisters on the train, and would continue to do so for the rest of the journey home. Little did happy-go-lucky Rita know, he mused, that it was suspicion of murder he had to avoid, not just the idle gossip of the over conventional. But she had the right idea.

So Percy was surprised when Rita telephoned him early next morning pressing him to come to the room she was sharing with her sister. It was after breakfast, and nearly time for the bus that was taking their party to the airport.

'Sweetie, our bags are going to be overweight,' she complained when he joined her. 'It's Kirsty's fault. Always buying heavy presents.' There was no sign of Kirsty: only Rita managing to look pert, sexy and dependent, all at the same time. She wrapped her arms around Percy's neck and kissed him warmly. 'Will you be an angel and take some of our stuff?' she pleaded, in a little-girl-lost voice.

'Of course. Anything for you. Give me whatever you want to get rid of,' Percy answered expansively. He had remarked to her on the ship how little luggage he had, even allowing for what he had kept of Sybil's belongings.

'Just that bag. Then we shan't be over the top.' She pointed to a smallish but expensive looking canvas hold-all, then glanced at the time. 'Hey, we'd better get moving.'

'It's locked,' said Percy, surprised that the bag weighed quite as much as it did. 'Shouldn't I have the key in case . . .?'

'Kirsty's got it. She's gone down already. She'll give it to you later. Don't worry, you won't need it. Oh, better put your name on the label.' She pushed a pen into his hand, and he scribbled on the shipping company's label she had tied to the bag handle. It was a similar label to the ones on his own bags. 'Now hurry, lover.' She kissed him again, but briefly this time, then pointed him toward the door.

He took the bag back to his room. Shortly afterwards the porter came and carried it down with the rest of Percy's things.

Since the girls were seated at the front of the bus, in keeping with his public appearance policy, Percy chose a place at the back, beside the safe Miss Mold.

One of the elderly male passengers, across the aisle, leaned over to say 'They're very hot on that here.'

'What?'

'Drug peddling.' The man pointed to the signs in several languages fixed at intervals along the luggage rack. In English the message read: WARNING. Drug trafficking punishable by death. Do not become involved – even innocently.

'How could anyone be innocently involved in carrying drugs?' questioned Percy.

'Nephew of a friend of mine was. Right here at the airport.' The other nodded authoritatively. 'He was a student with very little luggage or experience. Only seventeen at the time. Someone claiming to be overweight asked him to take one of his bags. The customs people opened it. It was a spot check.'

Percy had suddenly gone cold. 'What . . . what happened?'

'He was in gaol for months. In the end they believed his story and let him go. It was a close thing though.'

'Such a very nice hotel, wasn't it?' Miss Mold put in from the other side.

Percy answered with a brief affirmative, then fell silent for the rest of the journey. Was he being duped in the same way as the student? It would explain why Rita had been so especially nice to him. Despite his natural conceit, he hadn't truly convinced himself it had been solely male magnetism that had compelled her into his bed. Now there was a sickly feeling in the pit of his stomach that she had simply been setting him up.

'We said we wouldn't let people know we were together,' said Rita later, without looking at him and pretending she wasn't speaking to him either. He had caught up with her in the airport's moving throng.

'What's in the bag. Is it drugs? Heroin?' he whispered back.

'Of course not. Now get lost, will you, darling?' She increased her pace.

'Open the bag then. When we get to the ticket desk.'

Porters were bringing all the baggage on trucks from the bus. The passengers had been told to claim their own at the check-in. There were warnings all over the place about smuggling drugs – even sterner ones than those on the bus.

'Look at the warnings,' Percy insisted. 'I'm not taking that bag through. Not without seeing what's in it. Where's Kirsty? She's got the key you said.'

Resigned to acknowledging his presence at last, Rita pulled him aside toward a magazine stand. 'Kirsty's busy, love. I'm sorry you're like this. It's only a little thing you're doing for me. Quite safe. I'd have thought it was the least you could manage after the other night. And the rest.' She eyed him accusingly. 'They won't be stopping you. Not after your bereavement. It's a natural. Don't you see?'

'It *is* heroin. Oh my God.' He looked about him as if for help. 'Well I'm not doing it.'

She had her handbag open now, resting on the stacked magazines. 'I'm afraid you are, love. Did I show you the snaps?' The tone was relaxed. 'This one's so good of you and Sybil.'

'I tell you . . .' The new protest somehow became strangled in his throat. The print she had slipped into his hand showed Sybil half-way over the ship's rail with himself still holding her ankles. Both the faces were in full profile. He thrust the print into his pocket, while staring about wildly, terrified that someone else might have seen it.

'There's another one I took just before. Shows you bent down, catching hold of her legs,' Rita continued remorselessly. 'Don't worry, they weren't processed on the ship. I had them done overnight in Kuala Lumpur. The people who did them wouldn't have understood what was going on, even if they'd bothered to try. They're darkish exposures. I wasn't using flash. Just special film. The detail's all there though. The police wouldn't hesitate with these.'

'You're not going to . . .?'

'I am. Right now as well, if you're backing out on the bag. Play ball though, and you can have the prints and the negs after we're through customs in London. God's honour.

'But they hang you here for smuggling drugs,' he hissed desperately.

'Not always, love. And only if they catch you, which they won't. On the other hand, they'd definitely hang you for murder.'

Percy drew in a sharp agonised breath, as though he had been lanced somewhere sensitive. 'But you only get prison in England for . . . for doing either.'

'But you're out here, darling, aren't you? So you don't really have a choice, do you?' She watched the look of mute acceptance growing. 'So off we go then. And keep away from me till we're through. Oh, and if they do ask questions, don't try involving me or Kirsty, will you? If you do, we'd tell on you over Sybil straight off. Understand?' She closed her bag and walked away firmly.

He stood there trying to collect his thoughts and dully watching Rita disappear in the crowd heading for the check-in area. When he moved in the same direction, he was trying to pull himself together, wishing Sybil was with him, needing to ask her what he should do.

'Your things are over there, Mr Crickle.' Miss Mold never used Christian names. 'All right are you?' she added with concern. She was in front of him at the check-in desk.

'All right, yes.' He must be looking as guilty as he felt. He wiped his forehead, feeling the sweat streaming all over his body.

There were his bags all right, lying on the floor with some others still waiting to be claimed. Now the airline girl was holding her hand out for his ticket. He was just about to lift the bags on to the scales when the armed, uniformed customs official came over and stood behind him.

'With the cruise group, are you?'

'Yes. We're in transit.'

'These three yours?' Now the dark-skinned officer was leaning down reading the labels.

Percy hesitated. He knew he shouldn't have, but he couldn't help himself. 'Er . . . yes . . . They're mine.'

'British?' Without waiting for an answer the man selected a large printed card from a pack of them under his arm. The big printed words were in English, constituting a list of dutiable or prohibited items. 'You know the regulations?'

The list appeared as a blur before Percy's eyes. He swallowed. 'Yes.'

'You have anything to declare?' The small Malaysian looked bored not suspicious.

'No, nothing.'

'Could you open this one please?' He was pointing to the hold-all.

Percy's knees nearly gave out under him. 'Actually that one's not mine.'

'You said it was yours.'

'I made a mistake. I'm . . . I'm mixed up at the moment. I lost my wife, you see. She fell overboard. From the ship. Just a few days ago.' He was blurting out words desperately, knowing he was entitled to sympathy: the First Secretary had said so.

The customs officer was totally unmoved by the news of the tragedy. 'This bag please. Open it.'

Percy shook his head. 'I don't have a key. I mean that proves it's not mine, doesn't it?'

His expression unchanged, the man produced a big bunch of keys from his pocket.

'Mr Crickle has just gone through a very terrible experience.' Miss Mold offered from behind in the imperious tone of a senior ward sister protecting a defenceless patient.

'That's right. Like I said . . .'

'You want to unzip your bag?' The official interrupted. He had already opened the lock.

'It's not mine.' Slowly Percy undid the zip, his hand brushing the label inscribed with his name in his own handwriting.

Inside the bag a transparent envelope containing a photographic enlargement lay on top of a bright red cashmere wrap. The print that showed through the envelope was a coloured close-up of Percy and Sybil, posed smiling in deck chairs. In the photograph she was wearing the wrap, also the long chunky necklace that was also half-showing beside it in the bag.

The official looked at the print, then at Percy, then at the wrap and the necklace, and finally again at the label. Pushing aside the other items his hands burrowed deeper into the confines of the bag.

At that point it all became too much for Percy. He started sobbing uncontrollably.

'Fancy going all the way. Hanging him,' said Kirsty. It was six months since Percy's arrest in Kuala Lumpur Airport. She and the others were relaxing over drinks in a Los Angeles hotel room. They had reached California by different routes and already disposed of the drugs they had each been carrying. The evening paper carried the report of Percy's execution following the failure of a last minute final appeal.

'He deserved it,' said Rita.

'Have a heart, it wasn't his own powder. It was ours.'

'I meant for doing in Sybil. And for stupidity. He's properly spoiled the cruise ship into Malaysia ploy. We can't do a pick-up again that way in KL for years.'

Kirsty sniffed. 'But it still wasn't Sybil he was done for. Anyway, she was different. I'd have shopped him straight off for that. On the boat. It was your idea to use him instead. To carry an extra load. I was never sure. Neither was Gertrude, were you Gert?'

'Not of him, no. Only that he should have been looked after at the airport. By someone from the High Commission. Anyone bereaved like that should have been given VIP treatment. Diplomatic immunity. Escorted through customs and immigration.'

'Anyway Gert, you did your best for him.'

'Trying to protect our interests, that's all. It was a shame we lost the extra package. But he did take the heat off the rest of us. Even so, it shouldn't have been that way. He should have been escorted. I don't know what the British foreign service is coming to, really I don't.' Pausing to sniff, Miss Gertrude Mold then went back to her knitting.

DANNY GETS IT RIGHT

Michael Z. Lewin

Being Vice President is not nearly as time consuming as people seem to think.

Oh sure, I have to defend freedom and democracy, but not that many people die around the world. Not important ones. So I get time to try to be interested in things and to go places and to meet people. Geo thinks it's very important to get a feel for the common people so I do whenever I can.

And they appreciate it. Just last night, for instance, Wayne – he's one of our numerous bodyguards and very common – he said, 'Excuse me, sir, but Mrs Quayle asked me to remind you about going to *Swan Lake* tonight.'

'Gosh,' I said, 'it's a little on the cold side for swimming.'

Wayne laughed and said, 'Hey, you're grooved in there a lot more than people think, sir.'

And I laughed along and said, 'I do my best, Wayne.'

We go out a lot of nights, Maddy and me. In fact, there are a lot of misconceptions about the vice presidency. The time thing is only one of them.

Of course I had a lot of things going for me when I ascended to my high office. For one thing, Geo had already done a lot of vice presidenting so he could explain all the stuff he wanted me to do.

For another I already knew my way around Washington. I was a senator for eight years, remember, like Jack Kennedy.

Washington is not nearly as hard to learn your way around as a lot of people think. Of course I had an advantage there too. Way back years ago they hired the same guy to build Washington as built Indianapolis and he used the same plans. So I'll tell you a little trick I use. Whenever I have someplace to go in Washington, I just think of the name of the street it would be in Indianapolis and that way I know where it is.

But what you really want to know about is that murder I solved, isn't it?

Well, it was just one of the things that results from the fact that being Veep doesn't take all the hours that God sends, bless Him.

I mentioned the trip to *Swan Lake* already because I wanted to show that Maddy and I do a lot of social engagements. Although I don't have official duties at most of them, often as not people ask me to comment on one thing or another and because I am important they take a lot of notice of what I say. So even when I'm not being VP, I can't get away from it, if you know what I mean. So it's a full-time job all right. I may get a lot of spare time but it's not as spare as other people's.

Of course I do have a lot of specific jobs and not just to go to funerals or to generals in South America. I am in charge of the Senate and that helps me keep in touch with a lot of my old friends and use my influence. And I am head of the National Space Council. That takes some time.

Not that I know everything there is to know about space. Well, nobody does, do they? Space is a huge area. There's a lot of uncharted waters in space and one of our jobs is to draw a map of them. But I read about space when I get a chance and I get a lot of experts to read even more about it. Nobody expects me to know where all the streets are out there and I'm sure they weren't designed by that great guy who did Indianapolis and Washington. I mean, they were designed by God, of course. Now there *is* a great guy.

But I mentioned space because it's an example of how when I have to do something I don't know all about I get to have experts. In fact I have a lot of experts.

In fact I even have an expert on being vice president. That's Pete. He's a real talented young lawyer and he's a great guy and a friend of Geo's and of Jim Baker's. That's one of the things about being in this team. Everybody cares. Important guys like Geo and Jim take time from their busy schedules to show an interest in just about everything I say and do. Not that they're more important than me. Well, they are, but not in the fundamental kind of way because everybody is equal really, and that's one of the things that made this country great.

But they do care and that helps me care about them. Especially Geo, of course, because he's the one who took me out of Indiana and put me into the world. I really love the guy. Well, you know what I mean. It's OK for a guy to love a guy that way. I mean, I would really miss him if he was gone. I mean, for instance, if Geo died or something, well I just don't know what I'd do.

But the murder I solved, you want to know about that.

It began, I think I'd have to say, when Maddy and I went to this dinner at the Fortesques in Georgetown. I remember it because I had just been to track meet at Tucker's school and all the arrangements went wrong. First the camera crews got there late. Then my limousine, VP–1, wouldn't start so I had to catch a cab from the kids' school.

And I remember the taxi driver, a fully equal person of colour, and I talked to him, because it was a chance to talk to a common person and there also wasn't much else to do.

So I said to him, 'Hey, how about that deep doodoo Marion Barry's in?'

The driver didn't say anything at first, so I waited. He might have been a little confused – which often happens when I speak to common people. Or maybe he even hadn't heard about it, because not everyone watches television, you know.

But at the next red light he turned to me and he said, 'Did you hear the latest Dan Quayle joke?'

I was a little surprised, but I said, 'Hey, you know, I *am* Dan Quayle.'

'That's OK,' he said. 'I'll tell it slowly.'

But then the light turned green and I guess he can't drive and talk at the same time. Before long we arrived at the Fortesques.

Marilyn – that's Maddy, my better half, well, not better but equal but different half – she was already there. And as soon as Pete and I walked in the door Maddy and Wayne – he was guarding Maddy's body that day – they came over to me. And with them was another woman. Well, Maddy said, 'Oh Danny! The most terrible thing has happened.'

'What is it?'

'Robin Fortesque has had another stroke. He's dead.'

'He was in a wheelchair anyway, wasn't he?'

'Honey,' Maddy said, 'I'd like you to meet his daughter, Janine.' And she nodded to this other woman.

'How do you do, Mr Vice President?' the woman said, and she was a pretty cute lady for her age. Not that I would look at another woman than Marilyn, except when I was being introduced or something.

'I'm fine. How are you? Oh, sad I bet because of your Dad.'

'Yes,' she said.

'We first met Mr Fortesque last month,' Maddy said.

'That's right,' I said. I knew it was right, because Maddy's got a heck of a head for stuff like that.

'He told me,' Janine said. 'You made quite an impression.'

'Janine. That's an unusual name,' I said. 'Is it foreign? Not that there's anything wrong with that, of course. Some of the best names are foreign. Or at least they were.'

Geo taught me that: talk about them instead of yourself when you meet them. It's one of the little tricks that's good to do as Veep. He's one great guy, Geo and I'd really really miss him.

'We met in Milwaukee,' Maddy said. 'There was a convention for stroke victims that Danny was invited to.'

And then I remembered, there had been this big party with all these people in wheelchairs. I'd talked about wheelchair basketball and the technological advances that had been made and how good for the game it would be when they made wheelchairs that could jump.

'I remember,' I said. 'Your dad was the one whose wife kept giving him liquorice, wasn't he? That's your mom, right?'

'He certainly seemed to like his liquorice,' Maddy said, not without a certain pride in her spouse's memory.

But this lady Janine looked at me in the strangest way. In fact it was so strange I turned to Pete and whispered, 'Do I have a pimple on my nose or something?'

But before he could say 'No sir, Mr Vice President, sir,' or 'Yes sir, Mr Vice President, sir,' Janine grabbed me by the lapels.

Now Wayne was about to kill her when I said, 'It's all right, Wayne.'

You see, I didn't think that Janine meant it personally. And two deaths in one family on the same day would be a real shame.

Anyway she said to me, this Janine – and she was shouting – 'Did you say that my father's wife gave Daddy liquorice?'

'Yeah. Lots of it. In fact, he didn't eat anything else at this party, did he, Maddy? Even though it was a buffet and all the food was free and it was on a low table so guys like him could get at it. Isn't that right, Maddy?'

'Yes,' Maddy said. 'He ate a lot of liquorice.'

Then I said, 'I like liquorice all right even though it's black, but I wonder whether eating so much is good for a person.'

Well, at that, this woman Janine screamed. She did! A real scream. And she ran away.

'Boy,' I said, 'her daddy ought to teach her some manners.'

Of course people of foreign origination have different ideas of manners. That's one of the things you have to learn real fast when you're vice president. I remember Geo told me, almost first thing, 'Danny,' he said, 'you're going to have to get used to the fact that not everybody is like you.'

And it's true. You do have to get used to it.

Well this Janine had no sooner run away screaming than she came back leading this old guy by the arm.

'Tell him,' she said to me. 'Tell him.'

'Please don't shout at me, lady,' I said. 'You may be an orphan but that's no excuse to shout because I'm not deaf. In fact I don't allow anyone to shout at me unless they're my superior officers in the National Guard or members of the Cabinet. And,' I added stingingly, 'you aren't either one of those.'

'Tell him about Daddy and the liquorice!'

Pete whispered, 'That's the Surgeon General, sir.'

'Oh,' I said. I turned to the old guy. 'Sorry sir,' and I saluted. 'What was it I can do for you?'

'Janine has just told me that you saw her father being fed a lot of liquorice last month.'

'That's right.'

'Well spotted, Mr Vice President. I congratulate you.'

'Uh, thank you sir.'

Another thing Geo taught me was when someone congratulates

you, thank them. You don't get congratulated that often in life that you can afford to turn one down.

Then the General and Janine went away again.

I took Maddy to one side and I whispered to her, 'I know I am supposed to be friendly to everybody, but that Janine is really a pain in the neck, don't you think?'

But just about then I was introduced to the Botswana Ambassador, so I had to concentrate. In fact he looked like a chauffeur my Uncle Gene used to have. The chauffeur was pretty prickly so I said to this guy, 'I don't want to offend you, so maybe the best thing is for you to tell me up front just what kind of ambassador a Botswana Ambassador is.'

And that was the last I heard about Janine until I got the letter.

'Dear Mr Vice President,' it began. 'My stepmother got sentenced to life imprisonment this morning and I wanted to thank you.'

And then there was a lot of technical stuff. In fact, I was busy reading up on space and I thought about just sending a standard 'You're Welcome' letter but then Maddy came in and I showed it to her.

'Oh my,' she said.

That kind of annoyed me. Not in any significant way, because a love like ours is too strong for anything significant, but anybody can get annoyed sometimes. 'Your what?'

'Do you remember Janine Fortesque?'

Well, of course I did.

'She's written to thank you for telling her about the liquorice.'

'Oh,' I said. 'What about it?'

'Well Janine is a doctor.'

I hadn't realised that, but of course we are getting more and more foreign doctors over here these days.

'It turns out that what you said about her father being fed liquorice *proved* that his wife murdered him.'

'Murdered him? How?'

'With the liquorice.'

'They were only little pieces.'

'Being a doctor,' Maddy said, 'Janine knew that liquorice raises the blood pressure.'

'It does?'

'It's all here. Glycerrhizinic acid in the liquorice affects the adrenal gland and stimulates aldosterone production which promotes sodium absorption, hence fluid retention and elevated blood pressure.'

'Oh,' I said.

'Janine's stepmother was feeding Mr Fortesque liquorice in order to keep his blood pressure up so that he would have another stroke and die. And he did. And so the stepmother just got convicted of murder so Janine will inherit seventy-five million dollars.'

'Wow!'

'So Janine's written to thank you. Without you, her stepmother would never have been convicted.'

'Those stepmothers can really do it to you sometimes, can't they?'

'Danny,' Maddy said, 'you ought to let the world know about your part in bringing this murderer to justice.'

'Do you think so?'

'Definitely.'

So, world, that was the story. And boy, I'll tell you this: am I glad I never really liked liquorice all that much anyway!

THE TIGER'S STRIPE

Julian Symons

It began with the telephone call from Miriam. 'Bradley,' she said, 'there are some boys outside.'

Bradley Fawcett recognised in his wife's voice the note of hysteria that was occasionally discernible nowadays. It's the menopause, Dr Brownlow had said, you must be patient with her. So now his voice took on a consciously patient tone, a talking-to-Miriam tone it might have been called, although he did not think of it in that way.

'Friends of Paul's, you mean?'

'No. Oh, no. Beastly boys. Louts. They took his sweets.'

'Took his sweets,' Brad echoed stupidly. He stared at the contract on the desk in front of him.

'They asked him for them and he gave them one or two, and then they knocked them out of his hand.' She ended on a rising note.

Had she telephoned the office simply to tell him this? Patiently he said, 'Calm down now, Miriam. Is Paul upset?'

'No, he's – but they're outside, you see, they're still outside.' There was a sound that could have been interpreted as a kind of tinkling crack and then he heard her shriek, 'They've broken the glass!'

'What glass?'

'The living room – our beautiful living room window.'

Brad put down the telephone a couple of minutes later, feeling hot and angry. He had not rung the police because they would have come round and talked to Miriam, and he knew that would upset her. The window itself was not important, although he would have to put in a large and expensive sheet of plate glass, but this was not the first trouble they had had with hooligans in The Oasis.

Geoff Cooper's garage wall had been daubed one night with filthy phrases, and on another occasion the flowers in the middle of one of the green areas had been uprooted and strewn around as though by some great animal; on a third occasion the sandpit in the children's playground had been filled with bits of broken glass, and one little boy had cut his foot quite badly.

It was the senselessness of such acts that irritated Brad, as he said to his companions in the train on the way back from the city to Dunkerley Green. The journey was a short one, no more than twenty minutes, but there were four of them who always made it together. The trains they caught – the 9:12 in the morning and the 6:18 at night – were never crowded, and they preferred the relaxation of sitting in the train to the tension of driving through the traffic.

Geoff Cooper, Peter Stone, and Porky Leighton all lived in The Oasis, and they had other things in common. Cooper was an accountant, Stone ran a travel agency, Porky Leighton was in business as a builder's merchant, and Brad himself was one of the directors of an engineering firm. They all dressed rather similarly for going into the city, in suits of discreet pinstripe or of plain clerical grey. Porky, who had been a rugger international in his youth, wore a striped tie, but the neckwear of the other three was sober.

They all thought of themselves as professional men, and they all appreciated the civilised amenities of life in The Oasis. Brad, who had passed the age of fifty, was the oldest of them by a decade. He liked to feel that they looked to him for counsel, that he was the elder statesman of their little group. He felt the faintest twinge of annoyance that it should have been Geoff Cooper who mentioned the idea of a residents' committee. The others took it up so enthusiastically that it seemed incumbent on him to express doubts.

'Forgive me for saying it, Geoff, but just how would it help?'

'Look, Brad, let's start from the point that we're not going to put up with this sort of thing any longer. Right?' That was Porky. He wiped his red face with a handkerchief, for it was hot in the carriage. 'And then let's go on to say that the police can't do a damned thing to help us.'

'I don't know about that.' Brad was never at ease with Porky. It seemed to him that there was an unwelcome undercurrent of mockery in the man-to-man straight-forwardness with which Porky spoke to him.

'You know what the police were like when Geoff had that trouble with his garage wall.'

'Told me that if I could say who'd done it they would take action.' Geoff Cooper snorted. 'A lot of use that was.'

'The fact is, The Oasis is a private estate and, let's face it, the police don't mind too much what happens. If you want something done, do it yourself, that's my motto.' That was Porky again.

'Half the trouble is caused by television,' Peter Stone said in his thin fluting voice. 'There are programmes about them every night, these young toughs. They get puffed up, think they're important. I saw one this week – do you know what it was called? *The Tigers of Youth*.'

Geoff snorted again. Porky commented. 'You can tame tigers.'

'Nevertheless,' Brad said. It was a phrase he often used when he wanted to avoid committing himself.

'Are you against it? A committee, I mean,' Geoff asked.

'I believe there must be some other way of dealing with the problem. I feel sure it would be a good idea to sleep on it.'

Did he catch an ironic glance from Porky to the others? He could not be sure. The train drew into Dunkerley Green. Five minutes' walk, and they had reached The Oasis.

There were gates at the entrance to the estate, and a sign asking drivers to be careful because children might be playing. There were green strips in front of the houses, and these strips were protected by stone bollards with chains between them. The houses were set back behind small front lawns, and each house had a rear garden. And although the houses were all of the same basic construction, with integral garages and a large through room that went from front to back, with a picture window at each end, there were delightful minor differences – like the basement garden room in Brad's house, which in Geoff's house was a small laundry room, and in Porky's had been laid out as a downstairs kitchen.

Brad's cousin, an architect from London, had once burst into a guffaw when he walked round the estate and saw the bollards and chains. 'Subtopia in Excelsis,' he had said, but Brad didn't really mind. If this was Subtopia, as he said to Miriam afterwards, then Subtopia was one of the best places in England to live.

He had expected to be furiously angry when he saw the broken window, but in fact the hole was so small, the gesture of throwing a stone seemed so pathetic, that he felt nothing at all. When he got indoors, Miriam was concerned to justify her telephone call. She knew that he did not like her to phone him at the office.

'I told them to go away and they just stood there, just stood laughing at me.'

'How many of them?'

'Three.'

'What did they look like?'

'The one in the middle was big. They called him John. He was the leader.'

'But what did they –'

'Oh, I don't know,' she said impatiently. 'They all looked the same – you know those ghastly clothes they wear, tight trousers and pointed shoes. I didn't go near them. I called out that I was going to phone the police, and then I came in and spoke to you. Why should they *do* such a thing, Bradley, that's what I don't understand.'

She was the only person who called him by his full Christian name, and he had sometimes thought that it typified the nature of their relationship, without knowing quite what that meant. It always seemed, too, that he talked rather more pontifically than usual in Miriam's presence, as though she expected it of him.

'It's a natural youthful impulse to defy authority,' he said now. 'And when you told them you were going to call the police – why, then they threw the stone.'

She began to cry. It did not stop her talking. 'You're making it sound as if *I* were in the wrong. But I did nothing, *nothing*!'

'Of course you're not in the wrong. I'm just explaining.'

'What harm have we ever done to them?'

'No harm. It's just that you may find it easier if you try to understand them.'

'Well, I can't. And I don't *want* to understand.' She paused, and said something that astonished him. 'Paul knows them. They're his friends.'

That was not strictly true, as he discovered when he talked to Paul. They sat in the boy's bedroom, which was full of ingenious space-saving devices, like a shelf which swung out to become a table top. Paul was sitting at this now, doing school work. He seemed to think the whole thing was a fuss about nothing.

'Honestly, Dad, nothing would have happened. We were playing around and Fatty knocked the sweets out of my hand, and it just so happened that Mum had come to the door and saw it. You know what she's like – she let fly.'

'Fatty? You know them?'

'Well, they come and play sometimes down on the common, and they let us play with them.'

The common was a piece of waste ground nearby, on which Paul sometimes played football and cricket. There was no provision in The Oasis for any kind of ball game.

'Are they friends of yours?'

Paul considered this. He was a handsome boy, rather small for his thirteen years, compact in body and curiously self-contained. At least, Brad thought it was curious; he was intermittently worried by the fact that he could not be sure what Paul was thinking.

Now, after consideration, Paul replied, 'I shouldn't say friends. Acquaintances.'

'They don't sound like the sort of boys your mother and I would welcome as your friends.' Paul said nothing to this. 'You were playing with them this afternoon?'

It was all wrong, Brad felt, that he should have to drag the information out of Paul by asking questions. A boy and his father should exchange confidences easily and naturally, but it had never been like that with them.

By direct questioning, of the kind that he felt shouldn't be necessary, he learned that they had been playing football. When they had finished these three boys walked back with Paul to The Oasis. On the way Paul had bought the sweets. Why had they walked back? he asked. Surely they didn't live in Dunkerley Green? Paul shook his head.

'They live in Denholm.'

Brad carefully avoided comment. Denholm was a part of the city that he had visited only two or three times in his life. It contained the docks and a good many factories, and also several streets of dubious reputation.

It would have been against Brad's principles to say that he did not want his son going about with boys from Denholm. Instead, he asked, 'Why did they come up here with you? I don't understand that.' Paul muttered something, and Brad repeated rather sharply, 'Why, Paul, why?'

Paul raised his head and looked his father straight in the face. 'John,' said, "Let's have another look at Snob Hill".'

'Snob Hill,' Brad echoed. 'That's what they call The Oasis?'

'Yes. He said, "Let's see if they've put barbed wire round it yet".'

'Barbed wire?'

'To keep them out.'

Brad felt something – something that might have been a tiny bird – leap inside his stomach. With intentional brutality he went on, 'You live here. On Snob Hill. I'm surprised they have anything to do with you.'

Paul muttered again, so that the words were only just audible. 'They think I'm OK.'

Brad gripped his son's shoulder, felt the fine bones beneath his hand. 'You think it's all right for them to throw stones, to break windows?'

'Of course I don't.'

'This John, what's his last name?'

'Baxter.'

'Where does he live?'

'I don't know.' Paul hesitated, then said, 'I expect he'll be in The Club.'

'The Club?'

'They go there most nights.'

'Where is it?'

'East Street.'

A horrifying thought occurred to Brad. 'Have you been there?'

'They say I'm too young.' Paul stopped, then said, 'Dad.'

'Yes?'

'I shouldn't go there. It won't do any good.' With an effort, as though he were explaining, saying something that made sense, he added, 'You won't like it.'

In the time that it took to drive to Denholm, the bird that had been fluttering in Brad's stomach had quieted down. He was, as he often said, a liberal with a small 'l'. He believed that there was no problem which could not be solved by discussion round a table, and that you should always make an effort to see the other fellow's point of view.

The trip by car gave him time to think about his own attitude, and to admit that he had been a bit unreasonable. He could understand that these boys held a sort of glamour for Paul, could even understand to a certain extent their feelings about The Oasis. And just because he understood, it would be silly, it would even be cowardly, not to face them and talk to them.

Much of Denholm was dark, but East Street blazed with neon light. There seemed to be a dozen clubs of various kinds, as well as several cafés, and he had to ask for The Club. He did so at first without success, then a boy giggled and said that he was standing almost in front of it.

As Brad descended steps to a basement and advanced towards a wall of syncopated sound, he felt for the first time a doubt about the wisdom of his mission.

The door was open, and he entered a low-ceilinged cellar room. At the far end of it four boys were singing or shouting on a raised platform. In front of him couples moved, most of them not holding each other, but gyrating in strange contortions that he had never seen before except in one or two television programmes.

The atmosphere was remarkably clear. Well, at least most of them are non-smokers, he thought, and was pleased that he hadn't lost his sense of humour. He spoke to a boy who was standing by a wall.

'Can you tell me where to find John Baxter?'

The boy stared at him, and Brad repeated the question.

'John?' The boy gave Brad a long deliberate look, from face to shoes. Then somebody tapped Brad's shoulder from behind. He turned to face a fat boy wearing a purple shirt, jeans, and elastic-sided shoes.

The fat boy muttered something lewd.

His other shoulder was tapped. A boy with bad teeth grinned at him. 'You want the john?'

The first boy, not the fat one, tapped him, repeating the lewd remark.

The fat boy tapped him again. 'It's just looking at you. This way.' He walked slowly round Brad, staring at him. ''Cause we never seen nothing so square before, get it?'

As Brad looked at the clothes of the three boys around him, clothes that were different in several ways and yet were identical in the brightness of their shirts, and tightness of their jeans, and the pointedness of their shoes, he had the ridiculous feeling that it was he and not they who was outraging orthodoxy, that his neat dark suit and well-polished square-toed shoes were badges of singularity, the clothing of an outlaw.

The sensation lasted for only a moment. Then he shouted – he had to shout, because the tribal music rose suddenly to a louder beat – 'I want John Baxter.'

The boy with the bad teeth tapped him. 'You ask for the john, then you don't pay attention. I don't like that, not polite. I'm John.'

Brad faced him. 'You are? You're the John who –'

The fat boy said, 'You heard that, he said you're the john. You going to take that?'

The three of them had closed in so that they were now almost touching him, and he thought incredulously: they're going to attack me. Then a voice said, 'Break it up, come on now, break it up.'

The three boys moved back, and a stocky man with thick eyebrows and arms like marrows said, 'Whatcher want?' Brad found it hard to speak. The man went on, 'They're blocked. You don't want to get mixed up with 'em when they're blocked.'

'Blocked?' It was a new country, a new language.

'I'm here if there's trouble, but they're no trouble – it's you that's making trouble, mister.'

'I didn't – that's not true.'

'So they're blocked, they feel good, have fun, what's the harm? You don't belong, mister. They don't like you, so why don't you just get out?'

He could just hear himself say *all right, all right*. Then there was a small scream from the dance floor, and a girl cried, 'He hit me!' The bouncer began to push his way through the crowd on the dance floor.

Brad stumbled away, eager to go, and had almost reached the outer door when there was one more tap on his shoulder. He turned again, putting up his fists. A tall dark boy he had not seen before asked, 'Want me?'

The boy was dressed like the others, but there was something different about him – a kind of authority and even arrogance.

'You're John Baxter?'

'What do you want?'

Behind him was the fat boy who said now, with a hint of silly irrational laughter in his voice, 'He says he wants John, see, so we're–'

'Shut it, Fatty,' the dark boy said. The fat boy stopped talking.

'I'm Bradley Fawcett.'

'Should I care?'

'I'm the father of the boy –' He stopped, began again. 'You threw a stone and broke our window.'

'I did?' The boy sounded politely surprised. 'Can you prove it?'

'You did it, isn't that so? My wife would recognise you.'

'I tell you what,' the dark boy said. 'You got a suspicious mind. You don't want to go around saying things like that – might get you into trouble.'

A fair-haired girl came up, pulled at the tall dark boy's arm. 'Come on, John.'

'Later, Jean. Busy.' He did not stop looking at Brad.

In Brad's stomach the bird was fluttering again, a bird of anger. He said carefully, 'I believe you call the place where I live Snob Hill –'

The boy laughed. 'It's a good name for it.'

'I've come to warn you and your friends to keep away from it. And keep away from my son.'

Fatty crowed in a falsetto voice, 'Don't touch my darling boy.'

'Do I make myself clear?'

'John,' the girl said. 'Don't let's have any trouble. Please.'

The tall dark boy looked Brad up and down. Then smiled. 'We do what we like. It's a free country, they say, and if we want to come up to Snob Hill, see your son, we do it. But I'll tell you what – we'd like to make you happy. If you haven't got the money to pay for the window –' Brad raised a hand in protest, but it was ignored – 'we'll have a whip round in The Club here. How's that?'

He laughed, and behind him came the sound of other laughter, sycophantic and foolish. They were all laughing at Brad, and it was hard now to control the bird that leaped inside him. He would have liked to smash the sneering face in front of him with his fist.

But what he did in fact was to run up the steps to the street, get into his car, slam it into gear, and drive hurriedly away. It was as though some fury were pursuing him; but there was no fury, nothing worse than the sound – which he continued to hear in his ears during most of the drive home – of that mocking laughter.

When he opened the living room door their faces were all turned to him – Porky's, Geoff's, Peter's, eager and expectant. He stared at the three of them with a kind of hostility, even though they were his friends. Geoff was their spokesman.

'We were talking again, Brad, about that idea.'

'Idea?' He went over and poured whisky.

'The residents' committee. We all think it's pretty good, something we should have done a long while ago. We came to ask if you'd let us nominate you for chairman.'

'Brad!' That was Miriam, who had come in from the kitchen with coffee on a tray. 'Whatever are you doing?'

'What?' Then he realised that he had poured whisky for himself without offering it to his guests. He said, 'Sorry,' and filled their glasses. Porky was watching him with the ironical gaze.

'Hear you bearded the tigers on your own, Brad. How did it go?'

Miriam asked in a high voice, 'Did you see them? Are they going to pay for the window?'

'I saw them. They're louts, hooligans.'

'Of course they are,' Peter fluted.

'I told them some home truths, but it's impossible to talk to them. They –' But he found that he could not go into the humiliating details. 'They've got a kind of club. I saw them there, and I met the ringleader. I shall go to the police tomorrow morning.'

Porky stared at him, but said nothing. Geoff threw up his hands. 'You won't get anywhere with the police.'

Miriam came over to him. 'They will do something? Surely we've got a right to protection. We don't have to let them do what they like, do we? They frighten me, Bradley.'

'The best form of protection is self-protection,' Porky said, and expanded on it. 'We've got the nucleus of a residents' committee right here. We can easily get another dozen to join us, mount guard at night, look after our own properties. And if we find these tigers, we'll know how to deal with them.'

Miriam looked at Brad inquiringly. It seemed to him that they all waited on his judgement. Just for a moment a picture came into his mind – the picture of a tiger with the dark sneering face of John Baxter, a tiger being hunted through the gardens of The Oasis. Then the picture vanished as though a shutter had been placed over it. What was all this nonsense about tigers?

Brad Fawcett, a liberal with a small 'l', began to speak.

'I think we should be extremely careful about this. I'm not saying it isn't a good idea; I think it is, and I'm inclined to agree that it should have been set up long ago. But I do say we ought to think more carefully about ways and means. There are lots of aspects to it, but essentially it's a community project, and since you've been good enough to come to me, may I suggest that the first step is to sound out our fellow residents and see how many of them like the idea . . .'

As he went on he found that verbalisation brought him self-assurance, as it did when he got up to speak as chairman of the Rotary Club. He was not disturbed by the unwinking stare of Porky's little eyes, and if Geoff Cooper looked bored and Peter Stone disappointed, he pretended not to notice it.

They talked for another half hour and drank some more whisky, and by the time the others said good night, see you on the 9:12, the recollection of the visit to Denholm had become no more than a faint disturbance inside him, like indigestion. It did not become urgent again even when Miriam, gripping him tightly in bed, whispered, 'You *will* go to the police in the morning, won't you?'

Sleepily he said that he would – before he caught his train.

At 11:30 the following morning he was preparing with his secretary, Miss Hornsby, an intricate schedule for a conference to begin at noon. The conference was about the installation of new boilers, and his mind was full of maintenance costs when he picked up the telephone.

Miriam's voice asked, 'What did they say?'

For a moment he did not know what she was talking about, so utterly had he shut away that unsatisfactory interview at the police station. Then he remembered.

'The police? They seemed to think we were making a mountain out of a molehill. Perhaps they were right.'

'But what did they *say*?'

'They said if we could identify the boy who broke the window –'

'We can,' she said triumphantly. 'Paul can. He knows them.'

'They explained that it would mean Paul being the chief witness. He would be examined, perhaps cross-examined, in court. We don't want that, do we?'

In her high voice she said, 'I suppose not.'

'Of course we don't. At the moment he's taken it quite calmly. I can't think of anything worse than dragging him through the courts.'

'No.' There was silence. Miss Hornsby raised her eyebrows, pointed at her watch. With the note of hysteria in her voice, Miriam said, 'I'm sorry to bother you –'

'It's all right. I should have phoned you, but I've had a lot of work piled up, still have.'

'Isn't there *anything* the police can do?'

'I've told you what they said.' He was patient; he kept the irritation out of his voice. 'We'll talk about it later.'

'What time will you be home? Can you come home early?'

Still patiently, speaking as though to a child, he said, 'I have to go into conference at noon, and I don't know when I shall be free. I won't be able to take any phone calls. Pull yourself together, Miriam, and stop worrying.'

As he put down the receiver he saw Miss Hornsby's eyes fixed speculatively on him. He felt guilty, but what had he said that was wrong or untrue? Paul had been tremendously cheerful at breakfast, and had gone off in high spirits. As for the police, the Sergeant had as good as said they had more important crimes to worry about than a broken window. Brad sighed, and returned to the schedule.

He came out of the conference six hours later, feeling tight and tense all over. The client had queried almost everything in the estimate, from the siting of the boilers to the cost of the material used for lining them. He had finally agreed to revise the whole plan. Miss Hornsby had sat in, making notes, but when he got back to his room her assistant, a scared-looking girl, came in.

'Your wife telephoned, Mr Fawcett. Three times. She said it was very important, but you'd said nothing at all must be put through, so –'

'All right. Get her for me.'

'I hope I did right.'

'Just get her for me, will you?'

Half a minute later Miriam's voice, in his ear, was crying, 'They've got him, they've got him, Bradley – he's gone!'

'What are you talking about?'

'Paul. He's not come home from school. He's an hour and a half late.'

'Have you called the school?'

'Oh, yes, yes,' she cried, as though eager to get as quickly as possible through all such silly questions and force on him realisation of what had happened. 'I've spoken to them. He left at the usual time. I've been down to the common, he hasn't been there, I've done everything. Don't you see, Bradley, those boys have *taken* him. After you went to see them last night, this is their – their revenge.'

He saw again John Baxter's face, dark and sneering; he remembered the things that had been said in The Club; he knew that the words she spoke were true. Heavily he said, 'Yes. Leave it to me.'

'Bradley, what are they doing to my little boy?'

'He's my boy too,' he said. 'I'll get him back. Leave it to me.'

When he had hung up he sat for a moment, and felt the bird leaping in his belly again. You try to treat them decently, he thought, you try to be reasonable and discuss things with them, and this is what you get. They are like animals, and you have to treat them like animals. He dialled Porky Leighton's number.

Porky wasted no time in saying, 'I told you so.' He was brisk. 'This calls for action, old man. Agreed?'

'Yes.'

'Right, then. This is what we do . . .'

A thin rain was falling as they pulled up outside The Club. They grouped on the pavement, and Brad pointed down the steps. Porky led the way, the others followed. The door was closed, but it opened when Porky turned the handle. There was no sound of music inside and the room seemed to be empty.

'Nobody here,' Geoff Cooper said disgustedly. Then two figures came out from the other end of the room, behind the band platform.

Brad cried out, 'There he is.'

The four of them advanced on the boy. Porky brought him crashing to the floor with a rugger tackle. There was a short scuffle and then, in a moment it seemed, the boy's hands were tied behind his back.

The boy's companion launched herself at Porky. It was the fair-headed girl who had been with Baxter the previous night. Geoff and Peter held her. She was wearing jeans and a boy's shirt.

'Hard to know if it's a boy or girl,' Peter said. He put his hand on her and laughed on a high note. 'You can just about tell.'

The girl cried out, and Porky turned on Peter. 'Cut it out. None of that – you know what we're here for. We've got no quarrel with you, you aren't going to get hurt,' he said to the girl. He spoke to Baxter. 'You know why we're here.'

The boy spoke for the first time. 'You're off your beat, fatso. Shove off.'

They had gone to The Oasis before coming down here, and changed into the old clothes they wore on weekends for gardening or cleaning the car – clothes so different from their neat daily wear as to be in themselves a kind of uniform. Porky's thick jersey made him look fatter than usual. He was wearing gym shoes, and he balanced himself carefully on his toes.

'Just a few questions, Baxter. Answer them and we won't have any trouble. Where's the gang? Why is the place empty?'

'It's not club night.'

'Why are you here?'

'Cleaning up for tomorrow. What's it to you?'

Porky stuck his red face close to the boy's dark one, jerked a thumb at Brad. 'Know him?'

'That drip. He was in here last night.'

'You know his son. Where is he?'

Baxter looked at him with a half-sneer, half-smile. 'Tucked up in bed – would that be the right answer?'

Brad saw Porky's hand, large as a knuckle of ham, swing back and slap Baxter's face. The bird leaped inside him, throbbed so violently that his chest was tight. There was a ring on Porky's finger, and it had cut the boy's cheek.

'Not the right answer,' Porky said. 'The boy's been kidnapped. By your friends, while you've fixed yourself a pretty little alibi to keep out of trouble. We want to know where he is.'

'I'll tell you what to do.'

'What?'

Baxter sneered. 'Ask a policeman.'

The bird fluttered up into Brad's throat. He moved toward Baxter with his fist raised. He wanted to speak, but he was breathing so hard he could say nothing intelligible.

After that it was all dreamlike. He participated in what was done –binding up the girl's mouth so that she could not cry out, locking the basement door, bundling the boy out into the car; but it did not seem to him that Bradley Fawcett was doing these things. Another person did them – somebody who had been re-leased from Bradley Fawcett's habitual restraints. In this release there was freedom, some kind of freedom.

They had come in his car, and as he drove back he took a hand from the driving wheel and passed it over his face. He was not surprised to find the skin damp, cold, unfamiliar. He absented himself from the presence of the others in the car, and thought about Miriam – how she had clung to him when he returned, and had begged him to go back to the police.

No, we're going to deal with it ourselves, he had told her quietly and patiently, as he took off his city clothes and put on his weekend ones. Who were 'we'? Porky and the others who had come to the house last night.

'What are you going to do?'

'See them. Find out what they've done with Paul. Get him back.'

'You really think that's best?' Without waiting for him to say yes, she went on, 'You won't do anything to make them hurt Paul, will you?'

The very thought of Paul being hurt had made him feel sick and angry. 'What do you think I am?' he asked, and as he repeated the words he was aware that they were a question – and one to which he could provide no simple answer, as he could have done a few days or even a few hours earlier.

As he was leaving she had come up and held him close to her. 'It's all our fault, isn't it?'

'*Our* fault?'

'Something to do with us. People like us.'

He had stared at her, then disengaged her arms, and left the house . . .

They took the boy into the garage. His arms were still tied behind his back. The small cut on his cheek had dried. He made no attempt to call for help, or even to speak, but simply looked at them.

'All right,' Porky said. 'That saw bench over there is just the job, Geoff. Agreed?' He had brought in with him from the car a small leather attaché case, and now he took out of it a length of rope. Geoff and Peter bent Baxter over the saw bench.

'Stop,' Bradley Fawcett said. 'What are you doing?'

'He needs a lesson. All agreed on that, aren't we? Let's give him one. Here's teacher.' And now Porky took something else from the attaché case and held it up, laughing. It was a thick leather strap.

As the bird inside him fluttered and leaped and hammered on his chest trying to get out, Bradley Fawcett said in a strange voice, 'We must ask him first. Don't do anything without asking him again first.'

Porky's glance at him was amused, contemptuous, tolerant. 'We've asked already, but let's do it according to Hoyle.' Casually he said to Baxter, 'Where's Paul? What have you done with him?'

Baxter spat out an obscenity. 'If I knew, d'you think I'd tell you?' And he spat out another obscenity.

'Very nice.' Porky savoured the response almost with pleasure. 'You see what we're up against, Brad. He's a tiger. We must show him we're tigers too.'

Brad took no part in stretching the boy over the bench and securing his feet. Instead, he considered wonderingly the garage in which everything was stacked tidily – the mower in one corner with its small bag of spanners beside it; the hoe, rake, garden shears, standing in racks; the packets of grass seed and weed-killer on a shelf; Paul's canoe suspended by pulleys. Surely this was the apparatus of a harmless and a decent life?

Yet he knew that he would never again be able to look at these things without thinking of the intrusion among them of this boy with his insolent manner and his strange clothing – the boy who was now bent over the saw bench with his trousers down around his ankles and some of his flesh visible, while Porky stood to the right of him holding the strap and Geoff tucked the boy's head firmly under his arm.

Brad took no part, but he found himself unable to move or to speak while the bird leaped within him, was quiet, then leaped again in its anxiety to escape as the belt descended and a red mark showed on the white flesh. The bird leaped violently at the sight of that red mark and Brad jerked a hand up in the air – but what did he mean to say with that outstretched hand? Was it a gesture of encouragement or of rejection?

He wondered about this afterwards and was never able to know if the answer he gave was honest; but at the time he could not wonder what the gesture meant for the garage door opened, Paul stood framed in it, and Brad was the first to see him. Brad said nothing, but he made a noise in his throat and pointed, and Porky half turned and lowered the strap.

'Dad,' Paul said. 'Mr Leighton. I saw a light. What are you doing?'

In his voice there was nothing but bewilderment. He had his school cap on, he looked handsome and detached, as an adult might look who had discovered children playing some ridiculous secret game.

Bradley Fawcett ran forward, grabbed his son's arm and shook it, trying to shake him out of that awful detachment, and said in a voice which he was horrified to hear come out as high and hysterical as his wife's, 'Where have you been? What's happened to you?'

'Happened? I went to Ainslie's party. Ainslie Evans, you know him.'

'Why didn't you tell anybody? You've got no right –' He could not think what it was that Paul had no right to do.

'But I did tell – I told Mummy yesterday morning. She must have forgotten.'

Paul took his arm away from his father's hand. He was looking beyond Brad to where Geoff and Peter were untying John Baxter, who drew up his trousers. 'Why were you beating John? Have you kidnapped him or something? Is this your idea of a joke?'

Porky gave a short snarl of laughter.

Paul went on. 'It's something to do with that broken window, isn't it?' Now he faced his father and said deliberately, 'I'll tell you something. I'm glad they broke that window.'

'Paul,' Brad cried out. He held out his hand to his son, but the boy ignored it. Paul stood in the doorway and seemed about to say something decisive, irrevocable. Then the door closed behind him.

John Baxter had his trousers zipped. He looked from one to the other of them. 'It was assault. I could make a case out of it. If I wanted.'

'It was a mistake.' Geoff cleared his throat. 'I don't know about the others, but I don't suppose you'd say no to a fiver.' He took out his wallet.

Peter already had his wallet out.

Porky said, 'Don't be silly.' They stared at him.

'Have you forgotten who he is? He's the little punk who daubs garages and breaks windows. What are you giving him fivers for – to come back and do it again?' When he spoke to John Baxter, the cords of his thick neck showed clearly. 'You were lucky. You just got a little taste of what's good for you. Next time it might be more than a taste, eh, Brad?

'It's done now,' Brad said mechanically. He was not thinking of the boy, but of the look on Paul's face.

'Don't worry,' Baxter said. 'You can stuff your money. But next time you come our way, look out.'

'We won't –' Geoff began to say.

'Because next time we'll be ready for you, and we'll cut you. So look out.'

Then the garage door closed behind him too, and Porky was saying with a slight laugh, as he snapped his attaché case, 'All's well that ends well, no harm done, but you certainly want to be careful of what your wife says, Brad old man.'

The bird fluttered again within him, and he found relief in shouting, 'Shut up.'

Peter Stone fluted at him. 'I think you're being unreasonable. We were doing it for you.'

'Get out!' Brad held open the door. Outside was darkness.

'You're overwrought.' Porky was smiling. 'A good night's sleep's what you need, Brad old man.'

They walked away down the path, Porky with a slight swagger, Peter Stone with an air of being the injured party. Geoff Cooper was last. He gave Brad's arm a slight squeeze and said, 'You're upset. I don't blame you. See you on the 9:12.'

I never want to see you again; you have made me do things I never intended – things I know to be unworthy: those were the words he cried out in his mind, but they remained unspoken.

He stood there for some minutes after the sound of their footsteps faded, and looked at the light in the house which showed that Miriam was waiting to receive him in a gush of apologetic tears; and as he stood there he came slowly to the realisation that Porky was right in saying no harm had been done.

A young tough had got a stripe on his backside, and very likely it would do him good. And as for Paul, it was absurd to think that what he had seen would affect him, or their relationship, permanently.

Bradley Fawcett's thoughts drifted away, and suddenly he found that instead of being concerned with Paul he was reliving that moment in which leather struck flesh and the bird had leaped violently, passionately, ecstatically, within him.

As he dismissed these thoughts and walked over to the house and the lighted window, he reflected that of course he would catch the 9:12 in the morning. There was for him, after all, no other train to take.

OUR MAN MARLOWE

Mike Ripley

ACT 1

'Our man Marlowe,' said the head of Her Majesty's Secret Service, 'was one of the best agents we ever had. He did a particularly good job for us in France.'

'Cambridge man, wasn't he, sir?' asked Smillet, who was not.

'Yes. Recruited him myself.'

'Like the others,' said Smillet, though not softly enough.

'Cambridge has proved very useful,' said the head of the Secret Service ruefully. 'Of course he gave us problems. You have to expect them from someone like him. Highly intelligent, artistic, and an unhealthy fascination with religion and, at the end of the day, he preferred boys to women. It may have had something to do with his death.'

'I thought his killer was known to us, sir.' Smillet knew he was.

'In more ways than one. There is no doubt that Freiser knifed Marlowe. The lamplighters who found him say it had been made to look like a bar-room brawl. A fist fight followed by one fatal stab wound through the eye. The problem is, Freiser used to work for us too, and that's where it could get tricky. I want you to examine the case and bring me a reason why it happened. Put nothing on paper; just take as long as you need and then report to me in person. You have *carte blanche* to use who you need. The files will be made available to you. That's all.'

Smillet nodded politely and withdrew.

The head of Her Majesty's Secret Service eased himself from behind the wide oak desk and warmed his hands at the open log fire.

He spent a moment gazing out of his window at the early morning traffic already clogging the London streets below. Then he took an iron poker from the fire, its four-inch tip red and smoking, and plunged it into the wooden mug of ale his servant had left on the hearth.

A pox on current medical thinking. He had his own remedy for the plague.

ACT II

'God's blood!'

As he cursed, Smillet hopped to the street corner and steadied himself against the flaking plaster wall of a spice merchant's shop. He removed his right boot and shook it angrily. A dozen pieces of brown shell trickled out into the dust of the street.

'Acorns,' said Smillet to the man with him, pulling the boot back on over holed and threadbare hose. 'They cover the floors of the theatres with them to soak up the piss and the puke of the audience.'

'I thought the theatres were closed, Eminence, because of the plague,' said the man called Chandler meekly.

'They are, as far as the public are concerned, but it's still the place to find the damned players. Why can't the plague take a few actors? No one would miss them.' Smillet stomped his boot. 'And don't call me Eminence.'

'As your lordship pleases,' wheedled Chandler.

'Now where exactly is this alehouse, man? I have no intention of being in Southwark by the time the Watch comes round.'

'The very next street, my Lord.'

Chandler made to take Smillet's arm but drew back when he encountered Smillet's no-nonsense stare, but the officer was grateful for the informer's guidance. He would certainly have walked by the alley which led to the alehouse known as the Angel, an alley reeking of foul smells and seemingly inhabited only by a suspiciously plump black cat.

'This is the unworthy place, my Lord,' whined Chandler. 'An alehouse in name only for the scum of a landlord has to brew his own liquor as his credit is too poor even for the lowest of common brewers. And he brews beer using hops, which he buys from *Dutchmen*, not honest ale, and has brawled in the street with the ale-conner twice already this month . . .'

Smillet cut him off with a wave of a gloved hand. His one good ring, a ruby, showed off well against the fading green glove and caught the informer's eye.

'My Lord would be advised to hide such precious stones,' he whispered. 'This hovel is a den of Catholic cut-throats.'

'Catholics?' hissed Smillet, tugging at his gloved fingers.

'My Lord, that is why they call it the Angel. In the days before the Queen's noble father broke with Rome, this was a papist house, owned by the Church and named for the Virgin Mary. They still meet here even though the good and great King Hal . . .'

'Yes, yes, enough. You are sure that this is where you saw the man Freiser?'

'Yes, my Lord. I name Ingram Freiser as God is my . . .'

'We are not in court yet. You are sure you know Freiser by sight?'

'I have seen him before many times when performing a service – a very small service – for my Lord Walsingham, but the other man I know not.'

'This other man, the man you call the Poet, he is here today?'

Chandler nodded enthusiastically.

'Today and every day, my Lord. He sits and drinks and eats and writes. Writes poetry; long, long poetry.'

'Then we go in and we have a drink and you point him out to me, but say nothing.'

'Very well, my Lord, but . . .'

'But nothing. Just do as I say and you will be paid. And if you keep your tongue still, you will be paid the amount agreed once more, at the end of thirty days.'

'After you, your Eminence . . .'

The alehouse was as unappetising and the ale as undrinkable as Chandler had warned. But in the dim light from the few open shutters, Smillet got a good look at the man Chandler called the Poet.

He had taken a corner table and provided his own candles. Three quills, a flask of ink and a length of parchment occupied the parts of the table not covered in apple cores, lumps of bread and empty tankards. The Poet constantly tugged at a wispy beard and when he looked up from the parchment it was only to gaze out of the window. The only sound came from the scratching of his quill.

'That's him, my Lord,' whispered Chandler. 'That's the man who gave Freiser the money.'

ACT III

'Well, Smillet,' asked the head of Her Majesty's Secret Service, 'what have you found?'

It was September and the nights had drawn in. Smillet waited until a servant had finished lighting the tallow lamps and left before he cleared his throat and began his report.

'With your leave, sir, we know that our man Christopher Marlowe died on the thirtieth day of May. The hand that killed him was that of Ingram Freiser and it happened at the end of a bout of drinking and gambling in a house of ill-repute run by one Eleanor Bull of Deptford. So much is known about the where and how and who, but little is speculated on the why.'

Receiving a generous nod from his superior, Smillet continued.

'There are four obvious possibilities, sir – perhaps five.'

'Proceed, Smillet.'

'First, it was genuinely a tavern brawl. Marlowe was said to be drunk, as was everyone in the Bull house that day. He had already a conviction for street fighting and only last year was again bound over to keep the peace.'

'But you do not think it was so simple?'

'I report, sir, I make no conclusion.'

'Second?'

'That it was a quarrel between depraved lovers. Freiser had the same unnatural desires as Marlowe, though of course he came from an even lower station in life. Perhaps some betrayal, some sleight.

Men like that can be unpredictable, and they and their sort are
naturally secretive.'

'Hence their use as agents. Unlikely. Continue.'

'The fact that Marlowe was a spy. Perhaps Marlow's death was
paid for by enemies of the State. The French King? Perhaps the long-
suffering King of Spain.'

The head of the Secret Service allowed himself a smile at that.

'Vengeance among spies? No, theirs is an honourable profession
such as it is. Kill yes, but only if there is an immediate advantage.
Revenge as a motive? I don't think so. Not our – their – style. The
fourth possibility?'

'A plot within this country, sir.' And now the older man sat up and
took interest. 'Marlowe never actually took holy orders though he
had strong views on religion, sir. Radical views. Views which led to a
formal accusation of atheism being made against him by one
Richard Baines two days after his death. There is gossip that a plot
against our Church – and therefore our Queen – was being formed
and involved some of the highest in the land.'

'You mean Sir Walter Raleigh, I suppose?'

Smillet's jaw dropped. While he did not believe a word of the
rumour himself, he had thought it at least *fresh* gossip.

'Discount that one,' said the head of the Secret Service. 'Sir Walter
gets blamed for most things these days. You said a fifth possibility?'

Smillet recovered himself.

'The most incredible of all, sir. Marlowe was thought of as our
leading dramatic writer, but there are more knives looking for
shoulder blades in that business than there are in ours. I have proof
that Freiser met with and was paid gold by another of these theatre
scribes, a rival to Marlowe, anxious to establish himself if and when
the theatres re-open. He already has some following and with
Marlowe out of the way, can command higher prices for his work. I
have established that he is the son of a glove-maker from Stratford
and his name . . .'

'Yes, Smillet, I know his name. You do not go to the theatre, do
you?'

'No sir. I consider the players to be coarse, stupid, and almost as
crude as their audience.' He realised what he had said. 'Begging your
lordship's pardon, that is.'

'Granted. I like this fifth theory, Smillet, I like it very much.'

Smillet recovered his confidence.

'Shall I have the poet brought in for questioning?'

'No, I think not,' said the head of the Secret Service. 'Well, not in the usual sense. I will have him brought to me, but discreetly so that we may talk. I have a few suggestions for him.'

'Suggestions, sir?'

'Yes, Smillet. You may not think much of the theatre, but others do and some would have us believe it to be quite a powerful weapon when it comes to keeping the people happy. That great unkempt, crude, audience of yours – they like to be reassured from time to time. For example, they like to be reminded of past glories of battles and heroic deeds by kings and noblemen from the past. Especially if they happen to be the forebears of our beloved Queen, whose popularity has slipped somewhat since the Armada. I'm sure our poet friend – our ambitious poet friend – will understand we have the same interests at heart.'

Smillet realised his jaw had dropped again.

'Well done, Smillet,' said the head of the Secret Service. 'You have helped me make an important decision which might prove to be very beneficial to all of us. That will be all.'

London
St Michael's Day
Year of Our Lord 1593

Warning to Scholars:
With apologies to John le Carré, Caryl Brahms and S J Simon, this story is fundamentally unsound.

THE PERFECT ALIBI

Paula Gosling

'Two beers, Charley.'

It was a corner bar not too many steps from the precinct station, and the sergeant and the rookie, coming off an arduous tour, were in need of a little restorative refreshment. They carried their glasses to a booth and settled in with a sigh each, one tenor and brief, the other long, low and grateful.

'Gets worse every day,' said the sergeant.

'You said that yesterday, Sarge.'

'Yeah, and I'll probably say it tomorrow, smart-ass. So? I got my rituals, you got yours.' The sergeant's voice was filled with the gravelly sediment of many years service, and the rookie grinned.

There had been a rush of business just before they'd come off duty, to say nothing of a fist-fight breaking out between a man and wife, and a visit from Granny, who had been reporting the same B and E for fifteen years – lost, one diamond tiara (she was the *real* Princess Anastasia). The sergeant had a special report sheet he pulled out for her, like clockwork, and wrote everything down with a leadless pencil, going over the old words so many times that they were wearing thin in places. It was, he said, her only entertainment – and it allowed them to keep an eye on her, for she was frail, and lived alone.

There were a lot of people in this slum precinct that the sergeant kept an eye on. Currently, one of them was the rookie, who showed promise, but was inclined to be swept away by the excitement of it all. As far as he was concerned the sergeant was the font of all wisdom, and he was always ready to listen to another story. The sergeant was flattered by this, naturally, being a childless widower and lonely, but he saw it as his duty to select incidents that would instruct rather than amuse. One day this freckle-faced bundle of energy would be in charge of a case, and he didn't want to see it go down the toilet just because the kid forgot the basics. In some ways, the young man's good looks would be useful – nothing disarms a female suspect quite as much as a handsome arresting officer. The sergeant didn't have that advantage, being thick in the middle and thin on top. However, the evening stretched ahead, and for some reason, the boy was in the mood for more learning.

Many steps, the sergeant always told him, many careful steps make a case.

He was telling it to him again today.

'Take, for instance, the line-up,' he said. The rookie frowned with frustration. They'd had a line-up that morning, in an attempt to identify a mugger and, as happened so often, the witness hadn't been certain enough to make an identification.

'Waste of everybody's time,' the rookie complained.

The sergeant shrugged. 'People don't like to make mistakes, don't like to take responsibility. They see all them scowling faces, they get confused. But sometimes that works for us, too.'

'I don't see how,' the rookie said. 'A lawyer can really milk a failure to ID.'

'Sure. But I'm not talking about failure, here, I'm talking about a wrong ID altogether, see? Take, for instance, the Excelsior diamond robbery in '56,' the sergeant continued. The rookie, smiling, leaned back to listen. This was History. He hadn't even been *born* in '56, for crying out loud.

'Torn down now, the old Excelsior Building. Was over on Third and Oakland, I think. Or was it Third and Elm?' the sergeant mused. 'Anyway, it had a lot of . . . Fourth and Oakland, that was it. Fourth and Oakland.'

'Where the McDonald's is,' the rookie said, encouragingly. He knew the location, he was on the ball.

'Yeah, yeah, where the McDonald's is,' the sergeant agreed. The rookie nodded.

'The Excelsior Building,' he repeated, as if taking notes.

The sergeant looked gratified. 'Yeah. Right. Well, it had a lot of jewellery wholesalers and diamond merchants in it, the Excelsior, and one morning we get a call that one of the biggest, called the Excelsior Diamond Exchange, had been ripped off. So, over we goes, and the place is like an anthill, people running around and yelling, everybody scared to death and like that. See, the minute they come in and hear the Excelsior has been ripped off, they figure *they* been ripped off, too, so we got to go from office to office, the whole damn building this is, looking, checking, and like that, OK?'

'Yeah, I get the picture.' The rookie could see it, he really could, a wave of blue surging through the corridors, and the plainclothes dicks in those hats with the big brims they wore in the fifties, taking notes, talking out of the side of their mouths, the whole bit. Two years in the Academy and two years on the beat had not dimmed the rookie's childhood images. Now was now, now was a bitch, but then, *then*, cops were cops. The sergeant was rolling on.

'So we do our thing, and we get to this little guy named Samuels, *his* name I remember to the day I die, and he says to us he was working late planning to cut a big diamond – did you know they take weeks to figure out how to do it? – and he maybe sees the thief. Gives us a description. Right away we're lucky, because this description, it had to be Buddy Canoli. He had him cold, down to a scar on the back of his left hand, which he saw as Canoli was on his way up the stairs.'

'If this guy was in his office, how could he see somebody going up the stairs?' the rookie interrupted.

'He left the door open to get a breeze, it was hot, OK?'

'OK.'

'It was August.'

'OK! Summer, diamonds, Buddy Canoli. I got it.'

'Right. So we pull in Canoli. He's got spit for an alibi, so we put him in a line-up with some guys we pull in from the street plus a few cops for flavour, and what do you think?'

'Samuels identifies a cop?'

'No. No.' The sergeant looks disappointed in his protégé. 'He identifies one of the guys we pull in from the street, name of Whitney. Don't forget *that* name, either. Walter Whitney. Anyways, this guy is *like* Buddy Canoli, I give you that, tall and thin and a lot of dark curly hair, plus on the back of his left hand, he has a birthmark. Not a scar, but close enough, maybe for a nitwit like

Samuels, who swears this is the guy he sees going up the stairs the night before.'

'Swell,' sympathised the rookie.

'Yeah, right. Well, there we were, we had Canoli cold, we *knew* he did it, and he knew we knew, and he walks out laughing. I was burned. To add to which, you know the regulations, I got to check this poor guy Whitney's alibi out, right?'

'What regulations?' the rookie asked, nervously. Another one he must have missed.

'The one which states if a person is identified on a line-up, we got to check them out, is which one,' the sergeant told him, impatiently.

'Oh yeah . . . that one,' the rookie said, vaguely, trying to pin it down in his mind.

'Right. Well, obviously, this Whitney is pretty boiled about the thing himself, respectable guy and all that. It makes him nervous, it would make anybody nervous, but I get him calmed down. You know, have a coffee, stuff like that.'

'Yeah, sure,' the rookie agreed. Stuff like that he could do standing on his head.

'So, Whitney tells me he was home alone like ten million other people. He's separated from his wife, who's gone back to her mother in Chicago, he leads a quiet life, all that. Fine, I don't argue, I got no reason to doubt him, do I? He goes on his way, I pick up a phone, call the caretaker of his particular apartment building which I happen to know personally, ask is this Whitney on the up and up, very casual, and the caretaker . . . what do you think he says?'

'Whitney is a nutny?' the rookie suggested.

'Nah. But Whitney is not being a truthful person. Like he says, he lives alone, all that. Only Whitney *wasn't* home that night because the caretaker has to go up there about the air-conditioning which Whitney told him was broken, and when he goes up he gets no reply. Goes up twice, too.'

'Maybe Whitney was asleep.'

'Caretaker has a passkey. Went in, fixed the air-conditioner, no Whitney.' The sergeant looked triumphant.

'Jeez. So why was he lying?'

'Exactly what I want to know.'

'Yeah, right!'

'So, I go down to where this Whitney has an office, he's some kind of accountant, and I say, look, friend, you weren't home on the night in question, anything to say about that, and he gets very nervous again and he closes the door and asks me to sit down. Turns out he's shagging his secretary on the night in question, but he doesn't want to put it on the record because his wife is on the look-out for anything she can get on him for a divorce, which would ruin him financially. He points to a picture of the wife on his desk, and she is one mean-looking old broad, that's for sure. One of those thin hard mouths, you know, the kind that bites and hangs on for keeps?' The rookie nodded. They'd picked up a hooker the other day who'd had a mouth like that and had done exactly what the sergeant said. The marks were still on his arm. He looked at the sergeant warily, to see if he was kidding him about that, but the old man's eyes were misty with remembering, so he let it go.

The sergeant was continuing. 'Well, Mr Whitney, I says to him, we can be discreet. If you'd said that to me right away and explained, I could have saved some shoe leather. He apologises, asks me if I want to speak to his secretary and confirm it, and I say, well, OK, if you insist, and so he calls in this little redhead from the outer office and says tell this man about last night.'

The sergeant smiled. 'She was a cute little thing, name of Marylou Mason, and she blushes, which tells me nearly all I want to know right there, but she speaks her piece all right, and says, yes, they were together all night, so I say thank you, Miss Marylou Mason, and I come away and write up my report.'

'Is that it?' asked the rookie, finally, when the sergeant took time out to drink some beer.

'No,' the sergeant said. 'We keep on at the thing, but we can't get a hold on Buddy Canoli on account of no solid forensic evidence and no ID from friend Samuels, the nearsighted diamond king, and so the case stays open. We're stuck, we have to move on to other things, and gradually the subject fades away, so to speak.'

'Gee,' said the rookie. 'That was interesting.' His voice was bleak with disappointment.

'I ain't finished yet,' the sergeant growled.

'Sorry.' The rookie brightened again.

'Right. So a few months later, we got to do another line-up, and we pull in some guys from the street as usual, this was, I think, maybe November now. And guess who is third from the right?'

'Whitney?'

'No, *Samuels*, dumbo. But seeing him reminds me of the case, so to speak. Nobody IDs *him* for robbery, though. Damn shame, would have served him right. Point is, because the whole thing comes back to me, my mind is aware, you know? And the next thing is, I spot Whitney in a restaurant a few days later. Only he's thinner, so I don't recognise him at first. Especially wearing a five-hundred-dollar suit, when before it was thirty-seven-buck numbers off the rack. Well, he spots me and suddenly lunch is over. I say hello, Mr Whitney, to him, as he goes by, being a friendly type. He gives me the fish eye and goes out of the place like his ass was on fire.'

'Aha!' the rookie pounced on this as evidence of something sinister. He was nearly chewing hunks out of the beer glass, trying to second-guess the story. The sergeant sighed. Where do they get all this energy he wondered, and pressed on.

'Well, he goes off so fast, he forgets his coat, see? I notice the waiter pick it up and take it to the manager, so, being a swell guy, as you know, I decide to take it around to Whitney's office for him, as it's only around the corner. But it's not his office anymore, I discover. He's moved uptown, they tell me. So, uptown I go, 'cause I'm now stuck with this damned coat, and sure enough, there he is. Set up in some fancy office with a new secretary and all very nifty. He makes like he didn't see me in the restaurant, acts all surprised, very nervous, too, wants me to get out of sight. I don't like to be put out of sight, you know? I got my pride.'

'You bet.'

'So I look around, I get like, expansive, you know, just to needle the stuck-up bastard. I say, business must be good, this is nice. He says yes. You must have some pretty fancy clients, now, I say, not like the old days. Yes he says, and no, he says. He obviously wants me gone, so I figure what the hell. I say here's your coat and he says thank you, and that's it and goodbye.'

The rookie's eyes showed disappointment again. 'Is this going to be another one of your stories about how no matter how hard you work on something it never comes right?' he asked, suspiciously. 'Are you just building me up for the big let-down?'

'Would I do that?' the sergeant asked, his eyes twinkling.

'You did last week, said it was a salutary lesson,' the rookie grumbled. 'You got it in for me, I sometimes think. I'm not as dumb as I look.' He caught the sergeant's eye, and grinned. 'I know, I know – I couldn't be. OK, go on.'

'Right.' The sergeant leaned back. 'I thought to myself about this new office business, and the new suit, and the new secretary, even classier than the one before, and how it all must have cost him an arm and a leg, so I ask around, and what do you think? Seems that Whitney suddenly has a lot of money to spend a few months back. And this new money of his makes an appearance right after the Excelsior robbery. Hey! I begin to think, maybe – just maybe – that little weasel Samuels made the right identification after all! Maybe it wasn't Canoli who ripped off the Excelsior, but *Whitney*, instead.'

'Son of a bitch,' the rookie breathed.

'I tell all this to the Captain and he says follow it up, things being what they were and him not liking a big case dangling unfinished like it was. So I go around to Whitney's bank and say what about all this money in August? And they say what about it? And I say was it cash. And they say, no, it comes by cheque from some insurance outfit in Chicago, which stops me, cold. What can I say? Oh, I say. They tell me he's got three accounts now, one personal with his wife, one for the business, and one for what's left of this big lump of money, which ain't much, but they don't let me look at no details because I ain't got no court order, only nosiness and my badge.'

'Bastards,' the rookie growled.

'You got to go by the rules,' the sergeant said, pointedly, then relented. 'But that doesn't mean you have to go by the main road, either.' The rookie lit up. He knew the sergeant wasn't going to give up *now*.

The sergeant let his halo glitter for a moment, then went on. 'I went around to Whitney's apartment, which was as new and fancy as his office. I ask to speak to his wife. The guy on the Security desk, who happens to be an old cop I know, tells me Whitney's wife has left him, and I say, *again*? And he says as far as he knows this is the first time she goes, and now Whitney, the bastard, leads the life of

Riley with a new girl every week. He doesn't seem to think too much of Walter Whitney, and I decide maybe I should push this button a little. Well, I say, I don't blame Whitney for kicking up his heels after having a wife that looks like a bad-tempered anteater, and this is the right tack because my old friend gets real mad, all of a sudden, and I wonder what's going on, here? Mrs Whitney is a lovely girl, he tells me in a loud voice, and who should he proceed to describe to me but Marylou Mason, Whitney's old secretary.'

'No!' said the rookie, with highly satisfactory surprise.

'Yeah. My old friend gets pretty excited about it – I guess sitting at a security desk in the lobby of some fancy building all day is kind of boring, at that – and bangs his fist, even. He didn't deserve her, he says. Turns out she was nice to my old buddy, and looked a little like his granddaughter, you know? This kind of thing is a big help when you're pushing a witness, believe me. Anyway, he gives me her new address, which is a little dump on Nineteenth. I think maybe I'm lucky at last, and I go over there. Sure enough, it's little Marylou, and boy, is she sour on Whitney. I ask her about the alibi she gave Whitney for the night of the Excelsior job and eventually she breaks down and says it was all a lie.'

'Got him cold!' said the rookie, banging his own fist down on the table top and nearly knocking over his empty beer glass.

'Jesus,' said the sergeant. 'Don't *do* that, you'll give me a heart attack one of these days.'

'Sorry,' said the rookie, looking around to see if anyone had noticed. One had – the new girl from Records who was sitting in the corner with some other clerks. She was laughing at him. He turned his attention back to the sergeant and tried to look as if they were on to something big. 'Go on.'

The sergeant, who had seen the girl in the mirror at the back, and knew how the rookie felt about her, went on. 'So tell me the truth, I says to Marylou, all braced to hear about the robbery. "He wasn't with me," she says. "He went to St Louis to meet someone he told me would mean big money. I got the feeling it was some kind of fast deal with this 'insurance business' he was getting into."

'"What kind of business is that?" I asked her.'

'"I don't know, but there were some very funny people involved. He wouldn't let me stay in the office when he talked to them. I think they must have been criminals or something. He thought I was stupid, but I'm not. He was always talking big, like he was so tough and knew what was what. He said when he got back we could get married, and we would be on easy street. He always bragged about the important people he knew, but *I* never met any." You could see he'd cut her up pretty bad, emotionally, you know? Poor kid. I hate guys like that.'

'Me, too,' said the rookie.

'But I had to go on. Was it like he promised, I asked her, and she says yes and no. The money showed up, all right, and he married her quick enough, and put her into that fancy apartment, but that was it. Like he had her where he wanted her and so he wasn't interested anymore. He never talked to her, never took her anywhere or introduced her to anyone, expected her to stay home alone all day. She'd only lied for him because she thought he loved her, but now it seemed to her like the lie had been all he'd really wanted her for. Seemed to me, too. After a while, she says, there started to be other women and she couldn't stand that, so she ups and leaves. Didn't take anything with her, either, but what she stood up in. Marylou was a real nice girl. She's a grandmother, now, would you believe? I put her on to another retired cop I know ran a security firm and she married his son. Anyway, back then I ask her will she tell the truth about Whitney in court, and she says, sure, as far as she's concerned he's a rat and we can have him.'

'But a wife can't testify against her husband . . .' interrupted the rookie.

'Sure, she can, if she wants to,' the sergeant said. 'The law says that a wife can't be *forced* to testify against her husband. That's a big difference.'

'And had Whitney gone to St Louis that night?' the rookie asked, feeling this foray into jurisprudence wasn't getting them anywhere.

'Yeah, just like she said. She'd booked the ticket herself, using the name Mason, and drove him to the airport.'

The rookie's eyes lit up. 'Ah,' he said, with great emphasis. 'But did she actually *see him get on to the plane*?'

The sergeant's expression was a patient one. 'Yeah,' he said. 'She did.'

'Oh,' said the rookie. 'Damn. But why didn't Whitney just *say* he'd gone to St Louis the night of the robbery?'

'I'm coming to that, dammit. She waved him bye-bye at around six that night, and as far as she was concerned, that was where he had been, St Louis. That was what she had been lying for him about – going to St Louis. If she couldn't maintain the first lie for him, that they'd spent the night together say, because she was worried about her reputation or something, she could *still* give him an alibi because she'd seen him leave town, right? He had *two* alibis, one behind the other. He figured that was perfect.'

'Right,' said the rookie, but he sounded dubious, which pleased the sergeant.

'Yeah, right. How did he know he was going to *need* two alibis?'

'I was just going to say that.'

'I thought you were.' The sergeant smiled kindly. 'Because you know and I know that planes not only fly *into* St Louis – they also fly *out* of St Louis. He had plenty of time to turn around and come back – the Excelsior job wasn't pulled until around midnight.'

'And did he take another plane out?'

'As a matter of fact, he did. After I left Marylou, I called St Louis and confirmed that "Mr Mason" took a flight out almost immediately after he got in. Bingo. A few days later, we arrest Whitney. I get a commendation, and that's how the line-up can sometimes work for you, although not always the way you expect it will.'

'So you broke the Excelsior case all on your own?' the rookie said, much impressed. 'That's real good.'

The sergeant shook his head. 'Hell, no. Deakins and Brady broke the Excelsior case, got Canoli cold through a fence that traded the information in exchange for a light sentence.'

'But you said . . .'

The sergeant leaned forward and tapped the table. 'The trouble with you is, you don't listen. Many careful steps make a case. I had to check Whitney out because of a false identification. He lied, so I had to go on checking. He told me he lied because he didn't want to drag the girl into divorce proceedings. That was another lie. Marylou said he married her as soon as he got back from his trip to St Louis. A trip *in* that was just a blind to cover another little trip *out*. He came into a lot of money very soon after this second little trip, which happened to take place the night of the Excelsior job, which is how he happened to come to my attention in the first place by getting identified in the line-up the next day.' He was beginning to wheeze, slightly. 'I wouldn't have had to check him out, otherwise, would I?' The sergeant leaned back, waved to the bartender for another two beers, then watched the rookie expectantly.

The rookie was confused. 'But you said he didn't *do* the Excelsior job.'

The sergeant sighed. 'He didn't. Walter Whitney had a third and even more perfect alibi for the Excelsior robbery. At the time the diamonds were being lifted, he was in Chicago – murdering his wife.'

A SNAKING SUSPICION

H. R. F. Keating

Detective Superintendent Peters called out through his open office door.

'Hey, Sherlock, looks like I've got something for you.'

For the umpteenth time in his police career, Detective Inspector Miles Rudge wished he had never, back in his days as a probationary constable in the schoolboyish atmosphere of police college, said in the course of one of the long, rambling, inane conversations they had been apt to have there that his hero was Sherlock Holmes. Why hadn't he picked on a footballer or a pop star like the rest of them? Then the nickname would never have got attached to him and life would have been a lot simpler, however much Sherlock Holmes remained, in secret, his real hero and those marvellous stories stayed at his bedside.

He went into the Super's office and stood in front of the desk.

'Sir?'

'They've got a body over at Clipsham Street. Body in a locked room. Just your style, by the sound of it. It's the wife of a man who runs a shop hiring out creepy-crawlies to TV companies. Been poisoned. They claim. Something quick-acting, and no sign of how it got into her. I daresay the locals have got it all arsy-versy. A locked room, for Pete's sake. But it wants a look-see.'

'Very good, sir. And the name of the establishment?'

Play it straight, Miles told himself. Don't give the old devil the least handle for any more of his Sherlock Holmes cracks.

'Shop called The Speckled Band. Whatever that's supposed to mean.'

'It's a Holmes story. One of the best. Terrific.'

He could have bitten off his tongue. And the Super was quick to pounce. 'Should be right up your street, then, eh? So just nip over there and bring us back the baffling answer.'

'I might at that.'

He shouldn't have let himself be riled, he knew he shouldn't. But the Super had the knack of getting under his skin, and that stupid boast had come shooting out.

The Super's piggy little eyes gleamed. 'Want to bet, Sherlock?'

'Okay. I will.'

This was getting worse by the minute, by the second. How could he guarantee to bring back an answer when he didn't know the first thing about the situation?

'Right. What'll it be? A fiver? Or that not fancy enough for Sherlock Holmes?'

'Well, no, not really. Let's make it a bottle of brandy, just like the Great Detective kept in his rooms for fainting clients. A bottle of the best brandy.'

'All right. Why not? One bottle of the best brandy if you're not back here with that little matter all wrapped up before I push off home this evening.'

Out at the shop with the odd name of The Speckled Band, Miles found the victim was the young wife of the not-so-young proprietor, a man who actually had the same name as Dr Grimesby Roylott, the villain in the Holmes story. Only he wasn't a doctor and he didn't have that resonant forename. He was simple William Roylott, and he said he had called his shop The Speckled Band because he stocked snakes and someone had told him about the story. But he nevertheless looked as much a villain, if of a lesser breed, than the gigantic Dr Grimesby Roylott. He was, in fact, thin and stooping and had a dark, unshaven face which seemed twisted in a perpetual slight sneer. And he was quick to make clear what he had felt about his now dead wife.

'Good riddance,' he said, darting a challenging glance at Miles. 'Bloody bitch. Anything in trousers and she was panting for it.'

Steady, Miles said to himself. Just because the fellow hated his wife and has the same name as the Conan Doyle murderer, it doesn't mean he killed her. Stay cool. Get at the facts.

But the facts, as he began to gather them, did nothing to make the case against William Roylott look any less likely. To begin with it really did seem as if the murder was, as the Super had stated, a locked-room affair. Even if the room was not the barred and cut-off bedchamber of the Holmes story, but a small and rather sordid bathroom. Yet there could be no doubt that its door had been firmly bolted. The constable, summoned by William Roylott when, he had said, he could not make his wife hear and was afraid she had fainted or something, had had to charge the door three or four times before he had smashed it open. And the little room had no window, just a small ventilator.

When Miles saw the latter, he really began to wonder if he had not slipped into some sort of a time-warp. Dr Grimesby Roylott had sent a snake, 'a swamp adder, the deadliest snake in all India,' sliding through a ventilator and down a bell-rope to kill his first victim in her locked room. And in the shop below the flat here, what was there but glass-fronted cage after glass-fronted cage of snakes, along with spiders, huge and furry, and lizards of every hue, tongues flicking and darting.

Certainly, too, William Roylott's wife – she had been decidedly attractive, to judge from her almost naked body – showed every sign of death by poison. And by some substance that, introduced into the bloodstream, acted almost instantaneously. But there was no sign of any sharp object. Nor was there anything to be seen which she could have drunk from. The one tooth-mug was fluffy with old dirt. But it really looked, almost beyond possibility of doubt, that the poison had been administered while she was in this very room, with its locked door and no other means of entry.

The wretched girl had evidently been in the middle of making up her face, half-dressed in bra and panties. Her cosmetics were ranged on a shelf in front of the small, brown-stained mirror, together with a cardboard box of cheap costume jewellery. She must, in fact, have been in the act of screwing home her second mock-pearl earring when the snake –

He stopped himself. Come on, Miles, if this Roylott has killed in that way in the hope that no one will cotton on, there's going to be a twin-fanged puncture mark on the body. Find that, and then it'll be time to start thinking about snakes.

Take care. Don't muck anything about before the scene-of-crime boys get to work. But all the same have a damn good look. If I'm really going to take a bottle of VSOP brandy off that supercilious bastard, then I'm going to have to cut a few corners.

Making sure the constable who had been on guard at the scene was well out of sight, Miles set to and made a rapid survey of every inch of the dead girl's body. He tweaked away the bra. He lifted up the panties. He parted the mass of blonde hair on her head.

And he found nothing.

He bit his lip in frustration. Of course, it was possible that when old Doc Kynaston came to do the post-mortem he'd find some tiny, almost invisible mark. But a snake bite ought to be more easily seen than that. And, in any case, if this was going to be solved by Forensics, then bang would go his bottle of VSOP.

He pushed himself to his feet, saw that the constable was still standing at the foot of the stairs and that there was no sign yet of the scene-of-crime team. Then he knelt again and repeated his search.

With no better luck.

Yet it must be a snake. It must be.

He stood up wearily. And his eye fell on the ventilator that had first put the notion of a Speckled Band copycat affair into his head. Damn it, when you took a proper look at it, the thing was really too small to let a snake through. It was one of those tinny affairs with a sliding shutter to close it in the coldest weather. It was open now, all right, but the slits in it were surely too narrow to let even the most minute snake squeeze past.

Nevertheless, he went up to it, stood on tiptoe, and peered into the slits. Black. Not a sign of daylight on the far side.

So was it a false affair? Just like in The Speckled Band? Did it lead, in fact, not to the open air but down a small shaft into the shop below? The shop with its collection of possibly deadly reptiles?

He felt in his pocket for the Swiss Army knife he always carried, and with it prised off the ventilator's tinny cover. And there, just a few inches inside, was something completely blocking the hole. Did this mean his theory was wrong? *It is a capital mistake to theorise before one has data.* The Master's words came back to him with chill clarity. But at least see what it was that was blocking the shaft. It could be some part of this Roylott's plan.

He dug his knife blade in and twisted and tugged. Suddenly whatever it was came away in a shower of brownish debris. It proved to be a wad of newspaper. He picked it up from where it had fallen at his feet and glanced at it. There was a date at the top of one of the sheets, a date five whole years earlier. And now, through the hole where the ventilator cover had been, the light of day was plainly to be seen.

So the blockage was no more than something someone had stuffed there long ago to keep out the draught. Foiled again, Mr Sherlock Holmes.

And the scene-of-crime boys would be here at any moment now – and before long the smirk on the Super's face as he accepted a bottle of fine brandy that he would probably douse with bloody ginger ale.

Miles stood staring miserably down at the body on the floor with the mock-pearl earring the poor girl had been about to put on lying where it had rolled beside her.

And then it came to him, how it had been done. How William Roylott had done it.

He stooped in a flash and reached for the other earring already in the girl's ear. Just in time he stopped himself, dug in his pocket for a handkerchief, and, taking the utmost care, used it while he unscrewed the little pearly object.

And, yes, just as he had thought. There on the earlobe under the small metal pad of the screw-fitting was, not the double puncture mark of a snake bite, but a tiny spot of blood from a single small wound, and on the face of the clamping pad there was a tiny sharp projection, which no doubt the girl's ugly, jealous husband had smeared with the poison.

Detective Inspector Miles Rudge rose to his feet.

He should not have done it. But he could not resist it. As he had entered the Super's office, the man himself had been standing up behind his desk, probably preparing to go home – and early, too. But he had looked somehow just like a barman behind his bar.

Miles had gone up to him.

'Bottle of brandy, my man,' he had said. 'And make it VSOP.'

Crime waves